SPECTRUM®

Critical Thinking for Math

Grade 3

Published by Spectrum®
an imprint of Carson Dellosa Education
Greensboro, NC

Spectrum®
An imprint of Carson Dellosa Education
P.O. Box 35665
Greensboro, NC 27425 USA

ISBN 978-1-4838-3550-1

02-195207784

Table of Contents Grade 3

Check What You Know

Adding and Subtracting Through 2-Digit Numbers

Solve for each unknown. Write the addition or subtraction sentence you used to solve. Show your work.

1. Bailey needs to read 75 pages by the day after tomorrow. She read some pages today and has 30 pages left. How many pages did Bailey read today?

2. Ivan is going to visit his aunt. He travels 32 miles on Saturday. He travels 15 miles farther on Sunday than he did on Saturday. How many miles did Ivan travel on Sunday?

3. The Murphy Library has 52 computers. It has 29 desktop computers, and the rest are laptop computers. How many laptops does the library have?

Lesson 1.1   Finding Unknowns

You can find unknown numbers in an addition sentence by subtracting the given numbers.

? + 19 = 52

Begin with the sum and subtract the addend you are given.

	Rename 52 as "4 tens and 12 ones."	Subtract the ones.	Subtract the tens.

$$\begin{array}{r} 52 \\ -19 \\ \hline \end{array} \qquad \begin{array}{r} {\scriptstyle 4\ 12} \\ \cancel{5}\cancel{2} \\ -19 \\ \hline \end{array} \qquad \begin{array}{r} {\scriptstyle 4\ 12} \\ \cancel{5}\cancel{2} \\ -19 \\ \hline 3 \end{array} \qquad \begin{array}{r} {\scriptstyle 4\ 12} \\ \cancel{5}\cancel{2} \\ -19 \\ \hline 33 \end{array}$$

minuend
subtrahend
difference

Subtract to find the missing addends. Show your work.

After the family reunion, Javier washed 25 plates by hand in the sink. He also washed some cups. When Javier finished, he had washed 51 dishes. How many cups did Javier wash?

Of the 25 plates Javier washed, some were plastic and some were not. If 15 of the plates were plastic, how many were not plastic?

Lesson 1.1 Finding Unknowns

You can use a number line to find unknown addends in an addition problem.

$48 + ? = 64$

Begin your number line on the right side with the sum. Using tens and ones, count backward to the amount of the given addend.

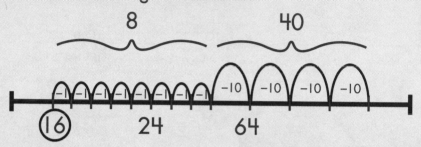

The number you end on is your unknown addend: $48 + 16 = 64$

Solve the problems. Use a number line to show your thinking.

Grace sells lemonade on the weekend. She sells 75 cups of lemonade on Saturday and Sunday. If she sold 13 cups of lemonade on Sunday, how many cup did she sell on Saturday?

Grace bought 36 lemons to make the lemonade. She used 23 lemons for Saturday's lemonade. How many lemons did she have left for Sunday's lemonade?

Lesson 1.1 Finding Unknowns

minuend – number in a subtraction problem that you are subtracting from
subtrahend – number in a subtraction problem that you are subtracting
(taking away)
difference – the answer in a subtraction problem

If the unknown number in a subtraction problem is the **minuend**, you can use addition to help you solve.

$? - 19 = 3$ To solve: $\begin{array}{r} 3 \\ +\ 19 \\ \hline 22 \end{array}$ So, $22 - 19 = 3$.	$? - 28 = 25$ To solve: $\begin{array}{r} 25 \\ +\ 28 \\ \hline 53 \end{array}$ So, $53 - 28 = 25$.

Solve the problems. Show the addition problem you used to solve.

Jakobi eats 25 grapes out of a bowl. 49 grapes are left. How many grapes did Jakobi have to begin with?

Riya is playing a video game. She loses 66 points on the second level. She has 116 points left. How many points did she start the second level with?

Lesson 1.1 Finding Unknowns

Solve each problem. Show the addition problem you used to solve.

John has a jar of candy. He shares the candy with his book club group and they eat 62 pieces of the candy. Now, there are 127 pieces of candy left in John's jar. How many pieces of candy were in John's jar to start with?

In her gymnastics competition, Hannah earned points for every event she competed in. However, the judges took away points as well. The judges took 41 points away from Hannah's total score. Hannah's final score was 92 points. How many points did Hannah earn before points were taken away?

Hannah's teammates scored 439 points in the gymnastics competition. How many total points did the team score?

Lesson 1.1 Finding Unknowns

If the unknown number in a subtraction problem is the **subtrahend**, you can use subtraction to help you solve.

$83 - ? = 17$

Subtract the smaller number from the larger number.

$$\begin{array}{r} {\scriptstyle 1\ 13} \\ 8\!\!\!/3\!\!\!/ \\ -\ 17 \\ \hline 66 \end{array}$$

$83 - 17 = 66$. So, $83 - 66 = 17$.

Solve the problems. Write the subtraction problem you used to solve and show your work.

Cindy had 34 tins of popcorn to sell. After a day of walking around her neighborhood and selling popcorn to all of her neighbors, she has 19 tins of popcorn left. How many tins of popcorn did Cindy sell?

If 12 of the remaining tins are filled with caramel popcorn, and the rest are butter, how many tins are butter popcorn?

Lesson 1.4 Adding and Subtracting in the Real World

Solve the problems. Show your work.

Brenda has a jar of gumballs. In the jar are 42 red gumballs and 27 yellow gumballs.

What is the total number of gumballs in the jar?

If Brenda removes 23 gumballs from the jar, how many will she have left? What is one possible combination of red and yellow gumballs left?

After removing 23 gumballs from the jar, Brenda adds 12 purple gumballs and 33 green gumballs. How many total gumballs are in the jar now?

Lesson 1.2 Checking Answers

You can use opposite operations to check the answer to an addition or subtraction problem.

Addition: 45 + 12 = 57
Check using subtraction: 57 − 12 = 45, and 57 − 45 = 12

Subtraction: 69 − 12 = 57
Check using addition: 57 + 12 = 69

Check each problem using opposite operations. Tell if the answer is correct. If it is not, give the correct answer. Show your work.

Anabel buys 15 tomato plants and 22 pepper plants. She thinks she has 15 + 22 = 38 total plants. Is she correct?

Mykal and Lin bought 68 party invitations and mailed out 46 of them. Lin says they have 68 − 46 = 22 invitations left. Is he correct?

Lesson 1.3　Opposite Operations on a Number Line

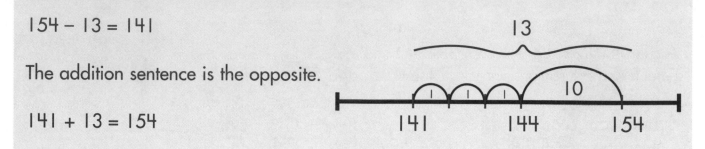

You can write a number sentence based on a completed number line.

154 − 13 = 141

The addition sentence is the opposite.

141 + 13 = 154

Write the correct addition and subtraction sentence for each number line given.

_____ + _____ = _____

_____ − _____ = _____

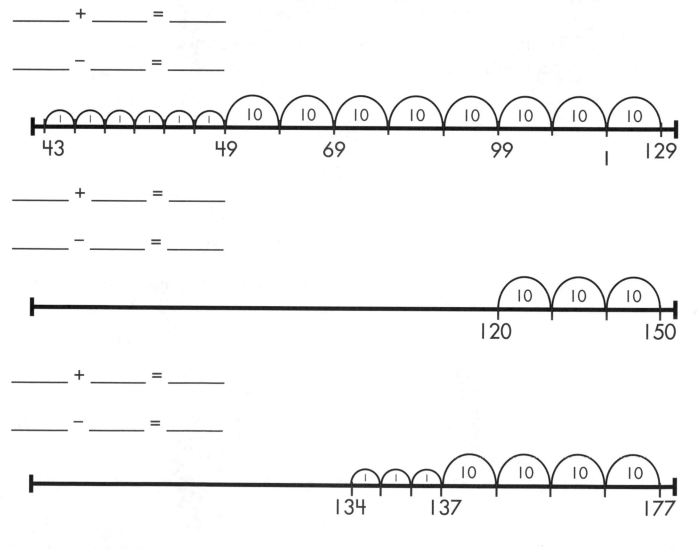

_____ + _____ = _____

_____ − _____ = _____

_____ + _____ = _____

_____ − _____ = _____

Lesson 1.4 Adding 3 Numbers

6 + 13 + 29 = ?
Begin with the first addend, 6. Count forward by tens and ones until you count your second addend. Write the number.
Then, count forward by tens and ones until you count your third addend. Write the number. The number you stop at is your answer.

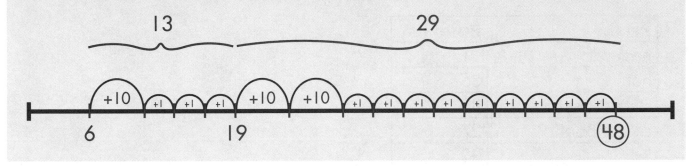

Solve each problem. Use a number line to show your thinking.

Mr. Dolby has 15 students in his class. Ms. Avila has 30 students in her class. Ms. Schmidt has 28 students in her class. How many total students are in the 3 classes?

In Mr. Dolby's class, 13 students turned in their homework. In Ms. Avila's class, 18 students turned in their homework. In Ms. Schmidt's class, 17 students turned in their homework. How many total students turned in their homework?

Lesson 1.5   Adding 3 Numbers in the Real World

Read each problem and solve. Write the addition sentence you used to solve and show your work under each question.

Marisa's school is holding a fall festival to raise money. Students can play games to collect points and win prizes. The table below shows which prizes students can claim and how many points are needed for each prize.

Prize	Points
necklace	11
hat	35
stuffed animal	39
sticker book	27
fish	42

Marisa's goal is to collect a necklace, a fish, and a stuffed animal. How many points does she have to earn?

Marisa's little brother has earned 98 points. What are 2 combinations of 3 prizes that he can choose?

Lesson 1.6 Unknowns in 3-Number Problems

To find an unknown addend in a 3-number addition problem, you must complete 2 steps of adding and subtracting to find your answer.

$13 + ? + 45 = 84$

First, add together the addends you are given: $13 + 45 = 58$

Then, subtract that sum from the total given:

$$\begin{array}{r} {\scriptstyle 7\ 14} \\ \cancel{84} \\ -\ 58 \\ \hline 26 \end{array}$$

The answer you get is the unknown addend: $13 + 26 + 45 = 84$

Solve each problem. Write the addition and subtraction problem you use. Show your work.

Jimmy has 64 square buttons in his button collection. Some of them are blue, 23 of them are red, and 25 of them are green. How many of Jimmy's square buttons are blue?

Jimmy also has buttons with other shapes. He has 45 oval buttons, 32 triangle buttons, and some buttons shaped like flowers. The total number of oval, triangle, and flower buttons is 107. How many buttons are shaped like flowers?

Lesson 1.7 Find the Unknown and Check the Answer

Alicia has 52 ice pops. She has 23 apple ice pops, some grape ice pops, and 11 cherry ice pops. How many grape ice pops does she have?

23 + ? + 11 = 52

23 + 11 = 34; 52 − 34 = 18; 23 + 18 + 11 = 52

18 of the ice pops are grape.

Now, check your answer with a number line.

Begin with 23. Count forward by tens and ones until you count the second addend. Write the number. Then, count forward by tens and ones until you count the third addend. Write the number. The number you stop at is the answer.

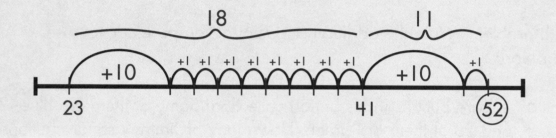

Solve the problem. Show your work. Check your answer using a number line.

Dante keeps his clothes in a closet. He has 9 pairs of jeans, 15 T-shirts, and some pairs of shorts. If Dante has 32 pieces of clothing in his closet, how many pairs of shorts does Dante have?

Check What You Learned

Adding and Subtracting Through 2-Digit Numbers

Solve the problems. Write number sentences to show your work.

1. 15 + _____ + 25 = 49

2. Jeremy has a dog-walking business. He walked 13 dogs on Friday, 16 dogs on Saturday, and 10 dogs on Sunday. How many dogs did Jeremy walk altogether?

Solve the problems. Use a number line to show your work.

Erin bought a roll of cloth 99 inches long. She gave her sister 72 inches to make a skirt. She gave her aunt 15 inches to make some headbands.

3. How much cloth did Erin give to her sister and aunt?

4. How much cloth does Erin have left?

Check What You Know

Adding, Subtracting, and Estimating Through 4-Digit Numbers

Solve. Show your work.

1. Lee Elementary School has 1,695 students. Davidson Elementary School has 1,523 students. At the beginning of every year, each student is given a student planner. About how many planners are needed at Lee Elementary School? About how many are needed at Davidson Elementary School?

2. If both schools buy 2,000 planners each, will they have enough planners to give 1 to each child?

3. Exactly how many planners will be left over after each student is given 1?

Lesson 2.1   Finding Unknowns

You can find unknown numbers in an addition sentence by subtracting the given numbers.

| | Begin with the sum and subtract the addend you are given. | The answer you get is the missing addend. |

$$\begin{array}{r} ? \\ +\ 1192 \\ \hline 9{,}057 \end{array}$$

$$\begin{array}{r} {}^{9}\ _{8}\cancel{10}15 \\ \cancel{9}\cancel{0}\cancel{5}\cancel{7} \\ -\ 1192 \\ \hline 7{,}865 \end{array}$$

$$\begin{array}{r} {}^{1\ 1} \\ 7865 \\ +\ 1192 \\ \hline 9{,}057 \end{array}$$

Solve to find the unknown number in each problem. Write the subtraction problem you use and show your work.

Irene and her sister decided to collect pennies over the weekend to donate to a local charity. Irene was able to collect 582 pennies. At the end of the weekend Irene and her sister had 923 total pennies. How many pennies did Irene's sister collect?

Of the 923 pennies that Irene and her sister collected, 444 of them needed to be cleaned. Out of the pennies Irene's sister collected, 20 pennies did not need to be cleaned. How many of Irene's pennies needed to be cleaned?

Lesson 2.1   Finding Unknowns

Find the unknown number in each problem. Write the subtraction problem you use and show your work.

_____ + 1,219 = 7,435

Kayla and Lamar are selling bracelets. So far, they have sold 1,255 blue bracelets, and some red bracelets. They have made some money from selling the blue bracelets and $5,028 from selling the red bracelets.

How many red bracelets have Kayla and Lamar sold so far if the total number of bracelets they sold was 3,769?

How much money have Kayla and Lamar made from selling blue bracelets if their total income so far is $7,538?

Lesson 2.1   Finding Unknowns

You can find unknown numbers in an addition sentence by subtracting the given numbers on a number line: $7{,}986 + ? = 9{,}232$

Start with the larger number at the right of the number line. Subtract by 1000s, 100s, 10s, and 1s until you reach the smaller number. Add together the 1000s, 100s, 10s, and 1s you subtracted to get the unknown addend.

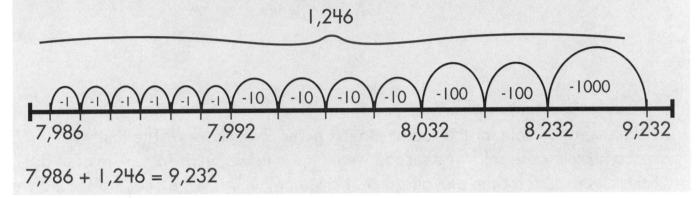

$7{,}986 + 1{,}246 = 9{,}232$

Find the missing addends. Show your work using subtraction on a number line.

The booster club sells raffle tickets at school events. At Saturday's soccer game, the booster club sold 681 total raffle tickets. 431 of those tickets were sold at the gate. The rest were sold at halftime. How many tickets were sold at halftime?

At the school musical, the booster club sold 314 fewer total tickets than it did at the soccer game. It sold 175 tickets at the door and the rest at the snack bar. How many tickets did the booster club sell at the snack bar?

Lesson 2.1   Finding Unknowns

Find each unknown. Show your work on a number line.

_____ + 211 = 414

Tickets went on sale for the soccer playoff game 2 weeks ago. The first week, 3,971 soccer tickets were sold. The second week, more tickets were sold. A total of 8,915 tickets were sold for the playoff game. How many tickets were sold the second week?

Of the 8,915 tickets sold, 4,502 were fans of the home team and the rest were fans of the visiting team. How many were fans of the visiting team?

Lesson 2.1   Finding Unknowns

If the unknown number in a subtraction problem is the minuend, you can use addition to help you solve: $? - 2,382 = 7,483$

Start with the difference and add the subtrahend:

$$\begin{array}{r} {\scriptstyle 1} \\ 7483 \\ + 2382 \\ \hline 9,865 \end{array}$$

The answer you get for the addition problem is the unknown value:

$$\begin{array}{r} {\scriptstyle 7\ 16} \\ 9\cancel{8}\cancel{6}5 \\ - 2382 \\ \hline 7,483 \end{array}$$

Solve each problem. Write the addition problem you used to solve.

On Thursday, the milkshake shop served 721 milkshakes, which is 142 fewer than it served on Wednesday. How many milkshakes did it serve on Wednesday?

On the other five days of the week, the milkshake shop served a total of 3,237 milkshakes. How many milkshakes did it serve for the entire week?

Lesson 2.1   Finding Unknowns

Find each unknown number. Write the addition problem you use to solve and show your work.

_____ − 792 = 6,736

Leigh does some research and counts how many pizzerias are in 4 different major cities. The following chart shows her results.

City	Number of Pizzerias
New York	3,112
Chicago	3,013
Boston	2,314
Philadelphia	1,890

How many more pizzerias are in New York than in Philadelphia?

What is the difference between the 2 cities with the most pizzerias and the 2 cities with the least pizzerias?

Lesson 2.1 Finding Unknowns

If the unknown number in a subtraction problem is the subtrahand, you can use subtraction to help you solve: $1,876 - ? = 894$

Subtract the smaller number from the larger number.

```
  0 1717
1,8̶7̶6
- 894
  982
```

The answer to the subtraction problem is the unknown value:

```
1,876
- 982
  894
```

Find each unknown. Write the subtraction problem and show your work.

Oliver buys 921 blueberries from the farmers market. He uses some to make pies for a bake sale at school. After he bakes the pies, he has 436 blueberries left. How many blueberries does Oliver use in the pies he bakes?

Oliver decides to use the leftover blueberries to make blueberry pancakes and blueberry muffins. He uses 226 blueberries in his blueberry pancakes. How many blueberries does he use to make his blueberry muffins?

Lesson 2.1   Finding Unknowns

Find each unknown. Write the addition or subtraction problem you used and show your work.

$5{,}473 - \underline{\hspace{1cm}} = 1{,}882$

Heather loves to travel. She travels 2,785 miles when she visits her grandmother. She travels 3,764 miles when she visits her best friend. She travels 1,985 miles when she visits her cousins. How many more miles does she travel when visiting her best friend than when she visits her cousins?

While visiting her grandmother, Heather's family decides to go on a trip to the beach, which is 533 miles away. When they go to the beach, has Heather traveled the farthest distance she has ever traveled? Why or why not?

Lesson 2.2 Checking Your Answer

Markus owns a hardware store. The cash register is broken, so Markus must add up the price of tools and building materials for customers. He also has to check his work to make sure he does not make a mistake.

Markus adds the price of a $567 jigsaw and a $295 drill to find a total of $862. Write and solve a subtraction problem to check his work. Is he correct?

Markus sold 2 hedge trimmers for $179 each. He solved $179 + $179 = $365. Write and solve a subtraction problem to check his answer. Is he correct? Explain.

Lesson 2.2 Checking Your Answer

You can use opposite operations to check the answer to an addition or subtraction problem with larger numbers.

Addition: $466 + 435 = 901$
Check using subtraction: $901 - 466 = 435$, and $901 - 435 = 466$

Subtraction: $801 - 148 = 653$
Check using addition: $653 + 148 = 801$

Check each problem using opposite operations. Tell if the answer is correct. If it is not, give the correct answer. Show your work.

Ms. Chan's class collected 323 cans of food for the school food drive. Mr. Okafor's class collected 345 cans. The students counted and said they had a total of $323 + 345 = 670$ cans. Were they correct?

Jessa saved $115 from her allowance and $160 from selling lemonade. She counted $115 + $160 = $275 that she could spend on a new computer. Was she correct?

Lesson 2.3   Real-World Addition and Subtraction

Solve each problem. Show your work.

Nellie sells tickets to events at her school. So far, she has sold 321 adult tickets and 262 children's tickets for a walkathon. How many tickets has Nellie sold for the walkathon? How many more total tickets would Nellie have to sell to reach her goal of 700 tickets sold?

Andrew works at an ice cream shop. He made a chart that shows how many scoops of ice cream he sold each day from Monday to Friday.

Monday	118
Tuesday	105
Wednesday	345
Thursday	126
Friday	612

On the weekend, Andrew sold 980 scoops of ice cream. How many more scoops did Andrew sell on the weekend than he did on Thursday and Friday?

Lesson 2.3 Real-World Addition and Subtraction

Solve the problems. Write the addition and subtraction sentences you used to solve. Show your work.

Students in the math club are selling two types of calendars. So far, they have sold 1,327 farm animal calendars and 3,915 puppy calendars. The students have made $2,534 from selling the farm animal calendars and $4,699 from selling the puppy calendars. How many calendars have the students sold so far? How much money have the students made so far?

The aquarium gift shop has a large collection of magnets. Dawson made the chart below to show how many magnets the gift shop has of several different animals.

Animal	Magnets
Dolphins	1,942
Sharks	6,413
Red Zebra Fish	4,120
Sea Turtles	2,817

How many more shark magnets does the gift shop have than sea turtle and dolphin magnets?

Lesson 2.4 Estimating Addition

You can use a number line to help you estimate addends in an addition problem.

Draw a number line and show the two closest tens to the addend.
Plot the number on the number line.
If the number is before the 5, it rounds down to the lower ten.
If the number is on or after the 5, it rounds up to the higher ten.

Add the rounded numbers together to get the estimated answer.

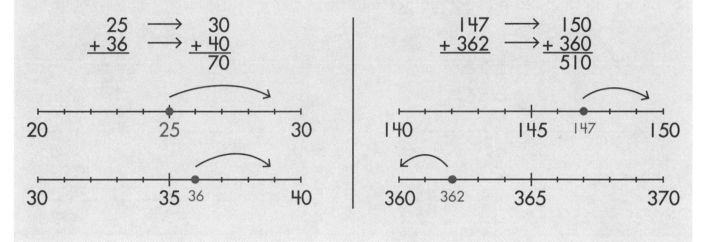

Use a number line to show how to round each addend to the nearest ten.
Then, solve.

57 + 51 =

357 + 603 =

Lesson 2.5 Estimating Subtraction

You can use a number line to help you estimate the minuend and subtrahend in a subtraction problem.

Draw a number line and show the two closest tens to the number.
Plot the number on the number line.
If the number is before the 5, it rounds down to the lower ten.
If the number is on or after the 5, it rounds up to the higher ten.

Subtract the rounded numbers to get your answer.

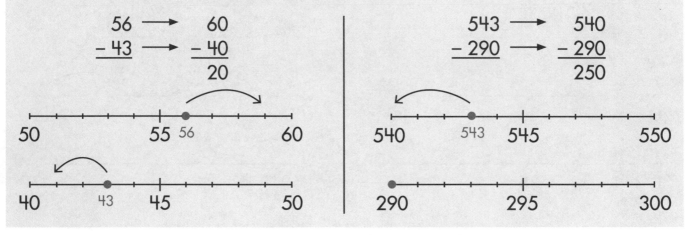

Use a number line to show how to round each addend to the nearest ten.
Then, solve.

80 – 45 =

943 – 457 =

Lesson 2.6 Estimating in the Real World

When adding, round each addend to place value that the numbers have in common.

$$
\begin{array}{r}
163 \\
+ \ 48
\end{array}
\longrightarrow
\begin{array}{r}
160 \\
+ \ 50 \\
\hline
210
\end{array}
$$

There are 78 musicians in the band and 32 singers in the chorus at a show. The principal wants to give every member of the band and chorus a flower at the end of the show. Estimate to find about how many flowers the principal needs to buy. Then, solve to find the actual number of flowers the principal needs to buy.

What is the difference between the exact number of flowers and the estimated number of flowers?

If the principal buys the estimated number, will she have enough flowers to give one to each musician and singer?

Lesson 2.6 Estimating in the Real World

When subtracting, round each number to the greatest place value that the numbers have in common.

$$
\begin{array}{r}
163 \longrightarrow 160 \\
-48 \longrightarrow -50 \\
\hline
110
\end{array}
$$

Sally is making jewelry for the school craft fair. She has 524 tassels, 2,008 small beads, and 96 large beads.

Sally makes a necklace that has 29 large beads on it. About how many large beads does she have left after making this necklace?

Can she make another necklace with 29 large beads?

Sally makes a necklace that has 214 small beads and 18 tassels on it. She makes another necklace that has 197 small beads and 13 tassels on it. About how many small beads and tassels does she have left after she makes both necklaces?

Lesson 2.6   Estimating in the Real World

Solve the problem. Show your work.

Two third grade classes collected about 900 soup can labels. Lucy's class collected about 300 more labels than Noah's class. How many soup can labels could Lucy and Noah's class each have collected to equal about 900?

Explain why Lucy's class could not have collected only 194 soup can labels.

_____

_____

_____

_____

_____

Check What You Learned

Adding, Subtracting, and Estimating Through 4-Digit Numbers

1. Jaime earned $195 during her first week of work. She earned $243 during her second week of work. She earned $122 during her third week of work. About how much money did Jaime earn after 3 weeks of work?

2. At the end of each week, Jamie had to pay $25 for her phone bill and $75 for her groceries. After she paid her bills, exactly how much money did Jaime have each week?

3. After she paid her bills, exactly how much money did Jaime have after 3 weeks?

Check What You Know

Multiplication and Division

1. Write the rule for the table below. Complete the table.

In	Out
6	12
7	
8	
9	18

Solve the problems. Show your work.

2. Luis bought 4 boxes of popcorn. Each box has 10 bags of popcorn. How many bags of popcorn does he have? Luis gives 2 bags of popcorn to his neighbor. How many bags of popcorn does Luis have now?

3. There are 10 buttons in each package. Patsy wants to buy 80 buttons. How many packages does Patsy have to buy? If each button costs 2 cents, how much money does Patsy spend on 80 buttons?

Check What You Know

Multiplication and Division

Find the unknown number in each problem. Write the division or multiplication sentence used to help you.

4. $45 \div$ _____ $= 9$

5. $72 \div$ _____ $= 8$

Solve the problems. Show your work.

6. Shane has 24 photos. He wants to arrange them in a rectangle on the wall above his bed. How many rows and columns could he use? Is there another configuration of the same numbers that Shane can use? If so, what is it? Write an equation to show the commutative property.

7. William has 10 friends. Each friend has 6 packages of gum. Each package of gum has 5 pieces. How many pieces of gum do William's friends have altogether? Use the associative property to solve the problem in 2 different ways.

Lesson 3.1 Understanding Multiplication Topics

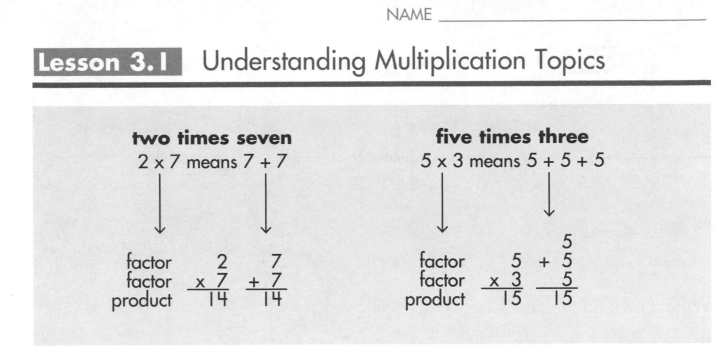

Write a multiplication problem and corresponding addition problem for each product given.

18   12

Carla has 4 bags. She puts 5 marbles in each bag. How many marbles are there in all? Write a multiplication problem and corresponding addition problem. Then, solve.

Lesson 3.2 Understanding Division Topics

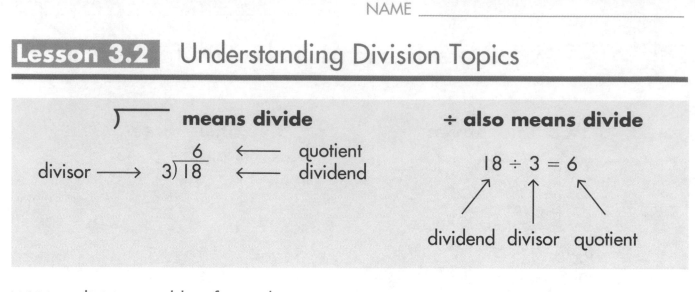

Write a division problem for each quotient given.

4   20

David earned $27 for mowing 3 lawns on Saturday. David earned the same amount of money for each lawn. How much did he earn for each lawn? Write a division problem. Then, solve.

Lesson 3.3 Multiplying Through 9 x 9

Multiply the number in each row by the same number in each column. Write the product in the box like the example given. Complete the whole table.

×	1	2	3	4	5	6	7	8	9
1									
2									
3			9						
4									
5									
6									
7									
8									
9									

Lesson 3.3 Multiplying Through 9 x 9

To complete a multiplication table, multiply each number in the **In** column by the same number to get the answer in the **Out** column.

Rule: Multiply by 3

In	Out
3	9
4	12
5	15

Rule: ?

In	Out
3	?
4	16
5	?
6	24

Sometimes, you have to find what the rule is by comparing the **In** and **Out** numbers given.

You can see that 4 x 4 = 16, and 6 x 4 = 24. So, the missing rule for the table above must be **multiply by 4.**

Determine the rule for each table given. Then, complete the table.

In	Out
6	30
7	35
8	
9	

In	Out
2	
3	18
4	
5	30

Rule: _____

Rule: _____

Lesson 3.4 Multiplying by Multiples of Ten

Use place value to multiply by multiples of ten.

9 x 40 = 9 ones x 4 tens   Multiply 9 ones by 4 tens.

9 x 4 tens = 36 tens = 360   9 x 40 = 360

Solve the problems. Show your work.

Justin read 3 books with 60 pages each. How many pages did he read in all? There were 4 additional pages in the back of each book telling about the next book in the series. If Justin reads those pages, how many total pages will he have read? Write the multiplication problem. Then, solve.

Wendy used up 4 rolls of stickers. If each roll had 30 stickers, how many stickers did she use in all? Write the multiplication problem. Then, solve.

Lesson 3.4   Multiplying by Multiples of Ten

Write a word problem to go with each multiplication sentence. Then, solve.

$60 \times 5 =$

_____

_____

_____

_____

_____

_____

$80 \times 5 =$

_____

_____

_____

_____

_____

_____

Lesson 3.5   Division and Multiplication

Multiplication and division are related to each other.

$$\begin{array}{r} 6 \\ \times\ 3 \\ \hline 18 \end{array} \longrightarrow \begin{array}{r} 6 \\ 3\overline{)18} \end{array}$$

$$\begin{array}{r} 5 \\ \times\ 2 \\ \hline 10 \end{array} \longrightarrow \begin{array}{r} 5 \\ 2\overline{)10} \end{array}$$

If $3 \times 6 = 18$, then $18 \div 3 = 6$.   If $2 \times 5 = 10$, then $10 \div 2 = 5$.

Write a division problem for each quotient. Then, write the corresponding multiplication problem.

24   18

There are 30 desks in the classroom. There are 6 desks in each row. How many rows of desks are there? Write the division problem used to find the answer. Then, solve.

Write the multipication problem you would use to find the number of desks in the classroom.

Lesson 3.6   Division Problems

Write a word problem for each division problem given. Then, solve.

$45 \div 9 =$

_____

_____

_____

_____

_____

$56 \div 7 =$

_____

_____

_____

_____

_____

Lesson 3.7　Finding Unknowns

To find the missing divisor in a division problem, divide the dividend by the quotient to find your answer.

$$14 \div ? = 7 \longrightarrow 14 \div 7 = 2 \qquad \text{Therefore, } 14 \div \mathbf{2} = 7.$$

To find the missing dividend in a division problem, multiply the divisor by the quotient to find your answer.

$$? \div 5 = 4 \longrightarrow 5 \times 4 = 20 \qquad \text{Therefore, } \mathbf{20} \div 5 = 4.$$

Find the unknown number in each problem. Write the division or multiplication sentence you used.

$54 \div ? = 6$ $\qquad\qquad\qquad\qquad\qquad$ $? \div 6 = 7$

Mrs. Shaw ordered 63 chairs and 7 tables for a banquet. Each table will have the same number of chairs. How many chairs will be at each table? Write the division and multiplication sentences used to solve this problem.

At the last minute, Mrs. Shaw had 9 more guests RSVP for the banquet. How many more tables and chairs will she have to order?

Lesson 3.7 Finding Unknowns

To find an unknown factor in a multiplication problem, divide the product by the known factor.

$$8 \times ? = 32 \longrightarrow 32 \div 8 = \mathbf{4}$$ Therefore, $8 \times \mathbf{4} = 32$.

$$? \times 4 = 32 \longrightarrow 32 \div 4 = \mathbf{8}$$ Therefore, $\mathbf{8} \times 4 = 32$.

Find each unknown factor by dividing. Write the division problem. Then, solve.

$7 \times ? = 49$ $? \times 8 = 72$

Fiona wants to buy 6 pieces of bubble gum. Each piece costs the same amount. If Fiona spends 30 cents for 6 pieces, how much did each piece cost? Write the multiplication sentence and the division sentence used to solve the problem. Then, solve.

Lesson 3.7 Finding Unknowns

You can find the unknown factor in a multiplication problem with a multiple of 10 by using place value to divide by multiples of 10.

$$? \times 4 = 280 \longrightarrow 28 \text{ tens} \div 4 \text{ ones}$$
$$28 \text{ tens} \div 4 \text{ ones} \longrightarrow 7 \text{ tens} = 70$$
$$280 \div 4 = 70$$
$$\text{Therefore, } 70 \times 4 = 280.$$

Find each unknown factor by dividing. Write the division problem. Then, solve.

$? \times 6 = 480$ $30 \times ? = 270$

There are 10 apples in each basket. Paige wants to buy 60 apples. How many baskets of apples does Paige have to buy? Write the division problem used to solve. Then, solve.

If each apple costs 3 cents, how much money does Paige spend on 60 apples?

Lesson 3.8 Multistep Word Problems

The PE teacher gave each team 6 basketballs and 6 tennis balls. If there were 5 teams, how many total balls did the PE teacher give out?

Each team gets 6 of each type of ball. I know that 5 times 6 is 30, so that is 30 basketballs and 30 tennis balls. Then, I can add the balls together, and 30 plus 30 is 60. So, there are 60 balls in all.

$$\begin{array}{r} 5 \\ \times\ 6 \\ \hline 30 \end{array} \qquad \begin{array}{r} 30 \\ +30 \\ \hline 60 \end{array}$$

Solve the problems. Show your work

9 girls and 6 boys each have an eraser collection. Each girl has 7 erasers in her collection, and each boy has 5 erasers in his collection. How many erasers altogether do the boys and girls have?

Brooke bought 8 boxes of chocolate chip cookies and 6 boxes of peanut butter cookies. Each box of chocolate chip cookies has 9 cookies. Each box of peanut butter cookies has 8 cookies. How many cookies does Brooke have altogether?

Lesson 3.8 Multistep Word Problems

Quincey earned 6 stickers a day for 9 days. After 9 days, he gave away 5 stickers to his best friend Tony. Then, he divided the rest of his stickers up between his 7 brothers. If each brother got the same number of stickers, how many stickers did each brother get?

James, Joseph, and Judd combined all of their toy cars. James had 21 cars, Joseph had 35, and Judd had 16. They wanted to donate an equal number of toys to 9 friends. How many toy cars did each friend get?

Hunter read 35 pages of his book on Friday and 52 pages of his book on Saturday. The book is 105 pages long. If he wants to finish the remaining pages in 2 days, how many pages must he read each day?

Lesson 3.9 Identity and Commutative Properties

Identity Property	**Commutative Property**
for addition: $3 + 0 = 3$	for addition: $3 + 2 = 2 + 3$
for multiplication: $3 \times 1 = 3$	for multiplication: $4 \times 3 = 3 \times 4$

A number sentence can change its look but not change its value.

$3 + 5 = 8$ **or** $3 + 5 = 4 + 4$ $3 \times 8 = 24$ **or** $3 \times 8 = 6 \times 4$

For each answer, write 2 different number sentences showing the identity property. Include at least 1 multiplication number sentence.

8

_____

_____

15

_____

_____

For each answer, write a number sentence showing the commutative property for addition.

18

_____

12

_____

For each answer, write a number sentence showing the commutative property for multiplication.

12

_____

18

_____

Lesson 3.10 Associative and Distributive Properties

Associative Property	**Distributive Property**

Associative Property

Addition:

$(1 + 2) + 3 = 1 + (2 + 3)$

Multiplication:

$(1 \times 2) \times 3 = 1 \times (2 \times 3)$

Distributive Property

$2 \times 7 = 2 \times (3 + 4) = (2 \times 3) + (2 \times 4)$

Solve the problems. Show your work.

Kevin and Leslie play a missing-number game. They write number sentences that have parentheses on both sides of the equal sign. They leave one number missing from each sentence.

Help Kevin find the missing number in Leslie's number sentence.

$(15 + 6) + 12 = (12 + 6) + \underline{\hspace{1cm}}$

Help Leslie find the missing number in Kevin's number sentence.

$(2 \times 2) \times \underline{\hspace{1cm}} = (2 \times 6) \times 2$

Write a number sentence that totals **81** to demonstrate the associative property.

Write 2 number sentences (addition and multiplication) that each total **64** to demonstrate the distributive property.

Check What You Learned

Multiplication and Division

1. There are 7 girls on stage. Each girl is holding 9 flowers. How many flowers are there in all? If 21 flowers are white, 21 flowers are red, and the rest are pink, how many flowers are pink?

2. During a tournament, 2 teams play against each other. There are 10 players on the field for each team. How many players are on the field during the game? There are 8 fields at the park where the tournament is held. How many total players are on all 8 fields?

3. Write the rule for the table. Complete the table.

In	Out
4	28
5	
6	
7	49
8	

_____

Check What You Learned

Multiplication and Division

4. 18 fish were caught on a deep-sea fishing boat. If each person on the boat caught 2 fish, how many people were on the boat?

5. Write the multiplication problem you would use to calculate how many fish were caught.

6. Shanette has 41 erasers, and Zoe gives her 7 more. Shanette gives each of her 8 friends an equal number of erasers. How many erasers does each friend get?

7. One of Shanette's friends does not want erasers and decides to divide hers among the 7 friends. Will she be able to do this? Explain your answer.

Mid-Test Chapters 1–3

Solve the problems. Show your work.

1. Pablo's favorite book is *Traveling Without Shoes*. The book has 845 pages of text and 79 pages of pictures. If Pablo is on page 514, how many more pages until he gets to the end of the book?

2. Vanessa is reading a book that has 692 pages. She reads 271 pages on Saturday and 287 pages on Sunday. About how many pages does Vanessa read on Saturday and Sunday?

3. Vanessa wants to finish the book on Monday. About how many pages will she need to read?

4. Ramsey took pictures of 64 animals at the zoo. He took 15 pictures of giraffes, 24 pictures of lions, and 12 pictures of pandas. How many pictures of other animals did he take?

Mid-Test Chapters 1-3

Solve the problems. Show your work.

5. Tyler went on a hiking trip. He started his trip at an elevation of 1,111 feet. After 3 days of hiking, he reached 6,389 feet. About how many feet did Tyler climb over 3 days?

6. If Tyler stopped to rest on the second day at an elevation of 4,220 feet, exactly how far did he climb the first 2 days?

7. How far did Tyler climb the third day?

8. Lola needs 415 balloons for a party. She has 179 balloons and her mom gives her 134 more. Does Lola have enough balloons for the party? If not, how many more does she need?

9. Write the rule. Complete the table.

In	Out
6	48
7	
8	
9	72

_____

10. Blake has 100 apples. She has 20 friends. She gave each friend 3 apples. How many apples did Blake give away?

11. It takes 10 apples to make a pie. How many pies can Blake make with the apples that she has left?

Eight friends want a new gaming system. The system costs $89. Each friend has $5.

12. Will they have enough money to buy the gaming system?

13. If they don't have enough, how much more do they need?

14. How many more friends with $5 would they need?

Solve the problems. Show your work.

15. There are 24 skiers waiting in line for the ski lift. 3 skiers can sit in each seat on the lift. How many seats are needed for all of the skiers?

16. If 1 skier decides to get out of line, how does this affect the number of seats needed for the skiers?

Abigail helps get 6 sailboats ready for a sailing class. She divides the supplies evenly between each sailboat. She has 12 sails and 30 life jackets. All of the sailboats need new ropes for their sails. Each boat needs 4 pieces of rope.

17. How many sails go on each boat?

18. How many life jackets go on each boat?

19. How many pieces of rope does Abigail need?

NAME _____

Check What You Know

Fractions

Divide each shape into the equal parts shown. Then, shade the fraction given.

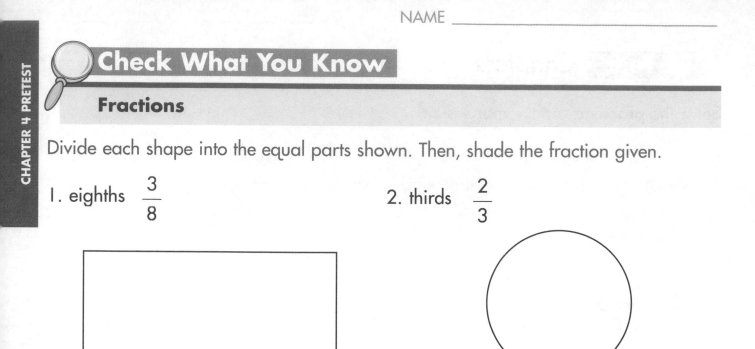

1. eighths $\dfrac{3}{8}$

2. thirds $\dfrac{2}{3}$

3. In Ms. Robinson's prize box, there are 7 toy trucks, 3 bouncy balls, and 6 yo-yos. What fraction of the prizes are toy trucks? If Ms. Robinson added 4 squishy fish, how would that change your answer?

4. Draw 2 ways to show $\dfrac{3}{4}$.

5. Write **<**, **>**, or **=** to compare.

$\dfrac{2}{3}$ ☐ $\dfrac{1}{2}$

Check What You Know

Fractions

6. Neil orders a pizza and eats $\frac{2}{8}$ of it. Luis orders another pizza and eats $\frac{4}{8}$ of it. Who has the most left over? Draw a picture to show your answer.

7. Draw and label the following fractions on a number line: $\frac{3}{8}$ and $\frac{8}{8}$.

8. Are $\frac{1}{2}$ and $\frac{1}{4}$ equivalent fractions? How do you know?

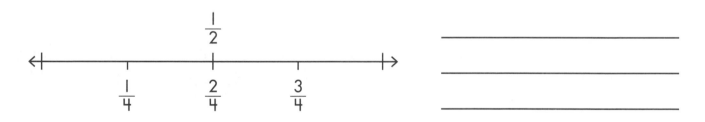

_____

_____

_____

9. Write the fraction as a whole number. Draw a picture to show your work.

$\frac{30}{5}$

Lesson 4.1 Parts of a Whole

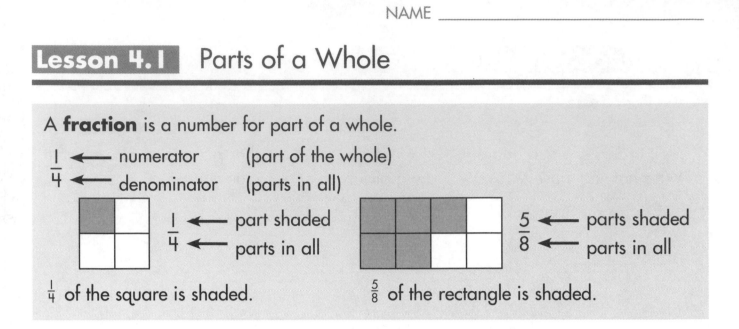

A **fraction** is a number for part of a whole.

$\dfrac{1}{4}$ ← numerator (part of the whole)
   ← denominator (parts in all)

$\dfrac{1}{4}$ ← part shaded
   ← parts in all

$\dfrac{5}{8}$ ← parts shaded
   ← parts in all

$\frac{1}{4}$ of the square is shaded. $\frac{5}{8}$ of the rectangle is shaded.

Draw 2 different shapes and divide each shape into fifths. Shade $\frac{1}{5}$ in one shape and $\frac{3}{5}$ in another shape. Write the fraction for the shaded portion under the shape.

Draw 2 different shapes and divide each into eighths. Shade $\frac{2}{8}$ in one shape and $\frac{7}{8}$ in another shape. Write the fraction for the shaded portion under the shape.

Lesson 4.2 Parts of a Set

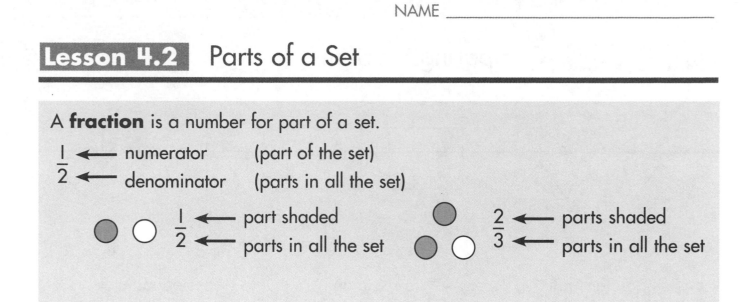

Draw 2 ways to show each part of the set.

$\dfrac{1}{3}$

Peter made a dozen cookies. 7 of the cookies had coconut and the rest had macadamia nuts. Draw circles to show the set. What fraction of the cookies had macadamia nuts? Shade the parts that show the fraction.

How would the fraction change if Peter made a second batch with the same number of cookies with coconut? Draw circles to show the set. Shade the parts that show the fraction.

Lesson 4.3 Comparing Fractions

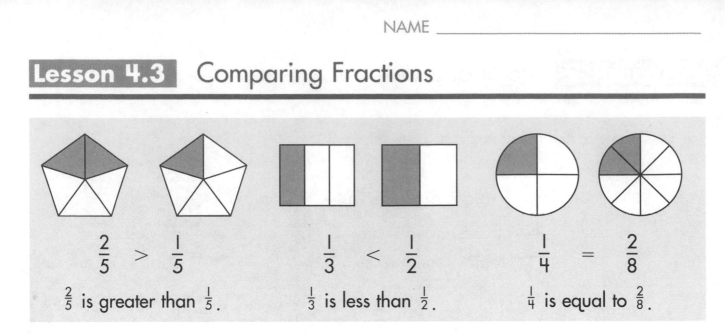

$$\frac{2}{5} > \frac{1}{5}$$

$\frac{2}{5}$ is greater than $\frac{1}{5}$.

$$\frac{1}{3} < \frac{1}{2}$$

$\frac{1}{3}$ is less than $\frac{1}{2}$.

$$\frac{1}{4} = \frac{2}{8}$$

$\frac{1}{4}$ is equal to $\frac{2}{8}$.

Draw the following fractions using circles. Then, write **>**, **<**, or **=** to compare.

$$\frac{1}{6} \bigcirc \frac{1}{3}$$

Nora has completed $\frac{3}{4}$ of her homework. Leo has completed $\frac{1}{2}$ of his homework. Draw and shade 2 squares to model the fractions $\frac{3}{4}$ and $\frac{1}{2}$. Which one is greater?

Lesson 4.3 Comparing Fractions

Write <, >, or = to compare.

$$\frac{1}{3} \bigcirc \frac{1}{2}$$

Three siblings each brought a chocolate bar to school. Melanie eats some of her bar at school and brings home $\frac{6}{8}$ of it. Matthew eats some of his bar at school and brings home $\frac{4}{8}$ of it. Madison shares some of her bar with friends and brings home $\frac{2}{8}$ of it. Which sibling brought home the least amount of leftover chocolate bar?

Three friends each baked pies for a picnic. After the picnic, Tasha had $\frac{1}{3}$ of her apple pie left, Ryan had $\frac{1}{2}$ of his banana cream pie left, and Victor had $\frac{1}{8}$ of his pumpkin pie left. Who had the greatest amount of leftover pie after the picnic?

Lesson 4.4 Fractions on a Number Line

Label $\frac{1}{8}$ on a number line.

First, divide the number line into 8 equal parts (the denominator).
Next, count from zero the parts you need (the numerator).
Finally, label the fraction.

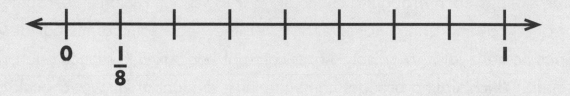

$$0 \qquad \frac{1}{8} \qquad\qquad\qquad\qquad\qquad\qquad\qquad 1$$

Mark and label the number line.

$0, \frac{1}{4}, \frac{2}{4}, \frac{3}{4}, 1$

The two number lines are divided into eighths. Circle the correct number line and explain why the other one is incorrect.

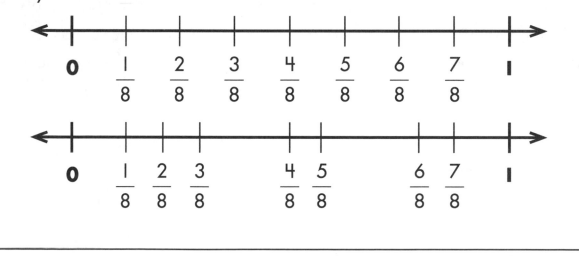

_____

_____

Lesson 4.4   Fractions on a Number Line

The fractions $\frac{2}{4}$ and $\frac{1}{2}$ are equivalent because they are at the same spot on the number line.

Write the equivalent fractions.

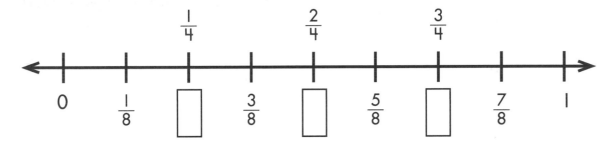

Complete the number line to show that $\frac{1}{3}$ and $\frac{2}{6}$ are equivalent.

Natalie says that $\frac{5}{8}$ and $\frac{1}{2}$ are equivalent. Is she correct? Explain. Draw a number line to show your thinking.

Spectrum Critical Thinking for Math
Grade 3

Lesson 4.5 Whole Numbers as Fractions

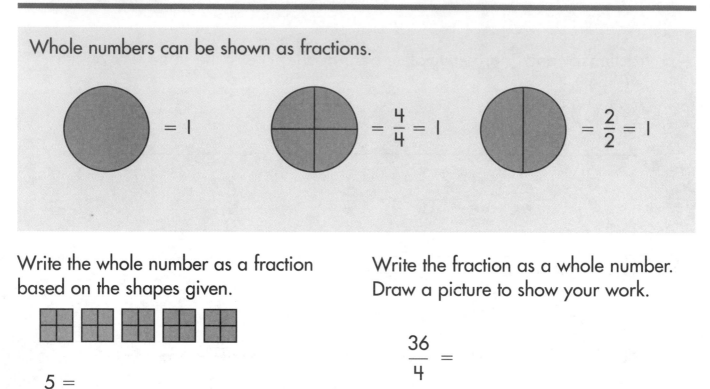

Whole numbers can be shown as fractions.

$= 1$ $= \frac{4}{4} = 1$ $= \frac{2}{2} = 1$

Write the whole number as a fraction based on the shapes given.

5 =

Write the fraction as a whole number. Draw a picture to show your work.

$\frac{36}{4} =$

Alexa baked 7 sheet cakes for a party. She divided the cakes into sixths. Write and draw a fraction that shows the amount of cake Alexa baked for the party.

Check What You Learned

Fractions

1. Divide the shapes and shade the fractions shown. Then, compare the fractions using **<**, **>**, or **=**.

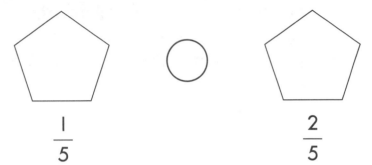

$$\frac{1}{5} \qquad\qquad \frac{2}{5}$$

2. Emmett has 3 pennies, 1 quarter, 2 nickels, and 2 dimes. What fraction of the coins are pennies? Draw circles to show the set. Shade the parts that show the fraction.

3. What fraction are quarters and dimes together?

4. Which is the larger grouping of coins: the pennies, or the quarters and dimes?

5. Show $\frac{3}{5}$ on a number line and in a set.

Check What You Learned

Fractions

Isabella and Jimmy both bring pies to the winter party. Isabella brings 2 apple pies sliced into sixths. Jimmy brings 3 pumpkin pies sliced into sixths. There are 2 pieces of pumpkin pie and 3 pieces of apple pie left over after the party.

6. Write a fraction to show how much pumpkin pie was eaten. Draw pictures to show your work.

7. Write a fraction to show how much apple pie was eaten. Draw pictures to show your work.

8. Jill has 4 rings, 3 bracelets, and 2 necklaces in her jewelry bag. What fraction of the jewelry is necklaces? Show the fraction of Jill's jewelry that is bracelets and rings on a number line.

Check What You Know

Measurement

Lauren and Maggie have a picnic at the park. They bring a basket filled with sandwiches and drinks. They also bring blankets to sit on. Lauren and Maggie get to the park at 1:45 P.M. and leave at 3:15 P.M.

1. Lauren's blanket is 3 meters long. Maggie's blanket is 4 meters long. How long are Lauren and Maggie's blankets altogether? Show your work.

2. Maggie wants to know how much the basket of food weighs. Should she use milligrams, grams, or kilograms to measure the weight? Why?

_____

_____

Complete the graphs.

3.
Favorite Outdoor Activity
Hiking = 30
Swimming = 45
Biking = 15

4.
Amount of Sleep for 3rd Graders
7 hours = 4
8 hours = 8
9 hours = 12

```
50
45
40
35
30
25
20
15
10
 5
 0
```

Amount of Sleep for 3rd Graders	

Key = _____

NAME _____

Check What You Know

Measurement

5. Michelle is placing foam padding in her dog's crate. The floor measures 3 feet by 4 feet. Draw a picture with unit squares to show the area of the crate's floor.

6. Explain how you would find the area without drawing unit squares.

7. Michelle wants to put a curtain up around the outside of the crate. Find the perimeter of the crate's floor to determine the length of the piece of fabric Michelle needs to buy for the curtain.

8. Stephen wants to paint 3 of the walls in his bedroom. Each wall is 9 feet tall by 10 feet wide. On each wall is a window that is 7 feet tall by 3 feet wide. How many square feet of wall does Stephen need to cover with paint?

Lesson 5.1 Volume and Mass in the Real World

Helpful Hint: A butterfly weighs about 1 gram.
A refrigerator weighs about 90 kilograms.
A dump truck can hold about 1,000 liters.

A juice bottle can hold about 2 _____.

A salt shaker holds 5 grams of salt. If there are 20 salt shakers in the restaurant, how many grams of salt are there in the restaurant?

Ellen weighed 4 kilograms when she was born. Now, she weighs 20 kilograms. How much weight has Ellen gained since she was born?

A computer's mass is 6 kg, and a printer's mass is 2 kg. A shop owner wants to place computers on the left side of the shelf and printers on the right side. She needs to keep both sides balanced. How many printers and computers should she put on the shelf?

Lesson 5.2 Drawing a Picture Graph

Three teams paddled canoes down a raging river. Finish the pictograph below to show how many miles each team canoes down the river.

Miles Canoed	
Team 1	 ⟍ ⟍ ⟍
Team 2	
Team 3	

Key = ⟍ = 20 miles

Team 2 rafted 60 miles. Draw the correct number of paddles on the graph above to show this.

Fill in the graph to show that Team 3 rafted 140 miles down the river.

How many more miles did Team 3 raft than Team 1?

Lesson 5.3 Drawing a Bar Graph

Use the chart to complete the bar graph.

June Weather	
Weather	Number of Days
sunny	14
windy	23
rainy	9
cloudy	17

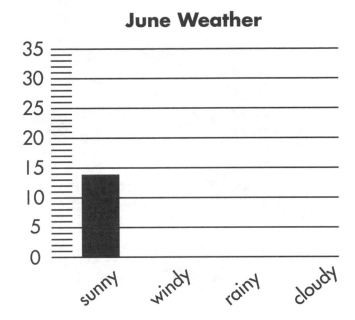

Explain why there are more days described in the chart than there are days in a month.

_____

_____

_____

_____

_____

Lesson 5.4 Gather Data to Draw a Line Plot

Use a ruler to measure the length of each object to the nearest quarter inch.

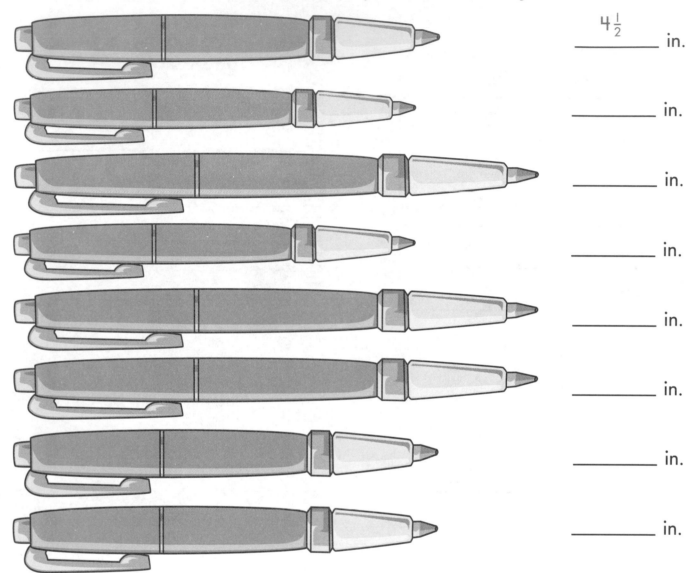

$4\frac{1}{2}$ _____ in.

_____ in.

_____ in.

_____ in.

_____ in.

_____ in.

_____ in.

_____ in.

Use the information above to fill in the line plot.

Pens Used in the Office

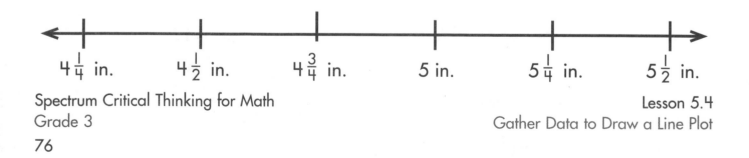

$4\frac{1}{4}$ in. $4\frac{1}{2}$ in. $4\frac{3}{4}$ in.   5 in. $5\frac{1}{4}$ in. $5\frac{1}{2}$ in.

Lesson 5.5 Finding Area with Unit Squares

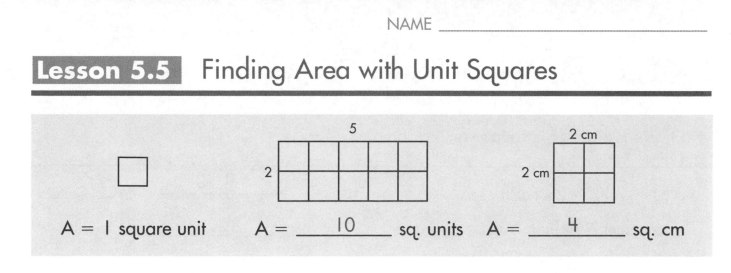

A = 1 square unit   A = ____10____ sq. units   A = ____4____ sq. cm

Draw the square units to find the area.

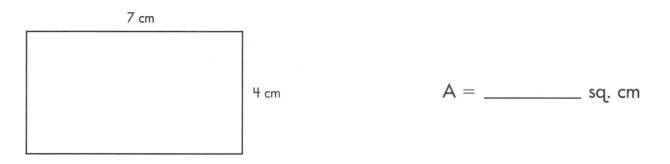

7 cm

4 cm

A = _____ sq. cm

Erica was covering her closet floor with tiles. The closet floor measures 4 feet by 3 feet. Draw a picture with unit squares to show the area of Erica's closet.

How many 1-foot by 1-foot tiles will Erica need to complete her closet?

If each tile costs $2, how much money will Erica spend?

Lesson 5.6   Area of Regular Shapes

To find the area of a square or rectangle, multiply length by width.

10 ft. × 2 ft. = 20 sq. ft.

The product is written as 20 square feet.

10 ft. (length)

2 ft. (width)

Orlando puts down 40 square feet of carpet in his rectangle-shaped bedroom. What could the dimensions of his bedroom be? Draw a picture and label it to show your thinking.

Denise wants to plant tulips, daffodils, and hydrangeas in a rectangular garden that is 30 feet long by 7 feet wide. The tulips should take up at least 30 square feet. The daffodils should take up no more than 35 square feet. The hydrangeas should take up 70 square feet. Denise also wants to leave a 1-foot-wide border around the edge of the garden. Draw a diagram to show one way Denise could design her garden.

Lesson 5.6 Area of Regular Shapes

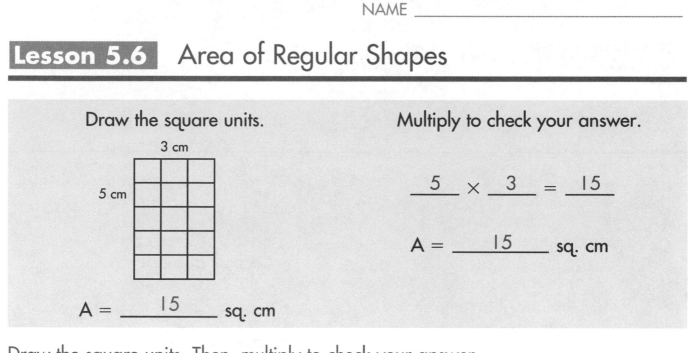

Draw the square units.

3 cm

5 cm

A = _____15_____ sq. cm

Multiply to check your answer.

___5___ × ___3___ = ___15___

A = _____15_____ sq. cm

Draw the square units. Then, multiply to check your answer.

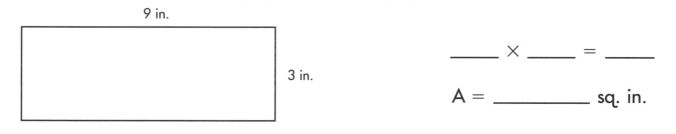

9 in.

3 in.

_____ × _____ = _____

A = _____ sq. in.

Sean wants to tile the kitchen floor. The kitchen floor measures 6 feet wide by 10 feet long. The tile store has high-grade tile, which costs \$8 per square foot; mid-grade tile, which costs \$5 per square foot; and low-grade tile, which costs \$3 per square foot.

How many 1-foot square tiles will Sean need to tile his kitchen?

How much will Sean pay for each type of tile?

Lesson 5.7   Area of Irregular Shapes

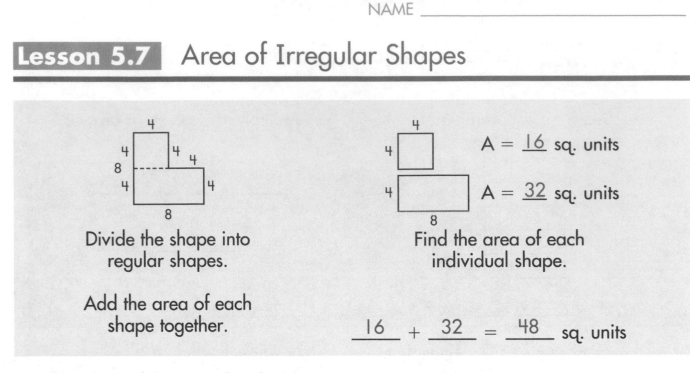

Divide the shape into regular shapes.

Add the area of each shape together.

Find the area of each individual shape.

A = _16_ sq. units

A = _32_ sq. units

_16_ + _32_ = _48_ sq. units

Find the area of the irregular shape.

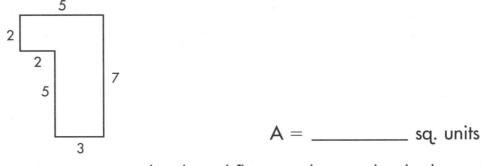

A = _____ sq. units

Carrie wants to put hardwood flooring down in her kitchen. Her kitchen is in the shape of an "L" shown below. Find the area of Carrie's kitchen to determine how much wood flooring Carrie will have to purchase.

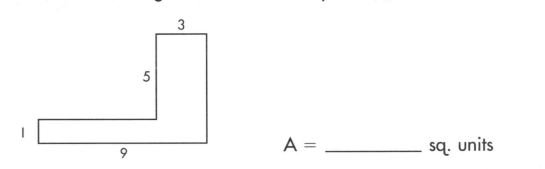

A = _____ sq. units

If the flooring costs $5 per square unit, how much will Carrie spend on wood flooring?

Lesson 5.7 Area of Irregular Shapes

Find the area of each irregular shape.

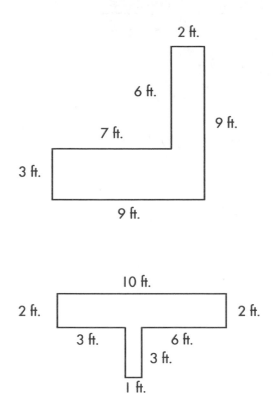

_____ sq. ft.

_____ sq. ft.

Donna has a closet shaped like the figure shown. What is the area of the closet?

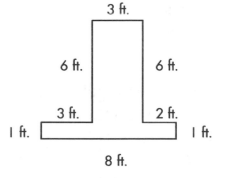

Donna wants to cover a 6-foot by 3-foot rectangle with carpet that costs $2 per square foot. She wants to cover a 1-foot by 8-foot rectangle with tile that costs $3 per square foot. How much money will Donna spend on flooring?

Lesson 5.8   Measuring Perimeter

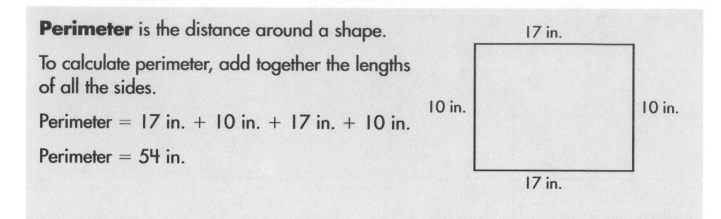

Perimeter is the distance around a shape.

To calculate perimeter, add together the lengths of all the sides.

Perimeter = 17 in. + 10 in. + 17 in. + 10 in.

Perimeter = 54 in.

Find the perimeter of the shape.

The total perimeter of this triangle is 225 yards. What is the value of the missing side?

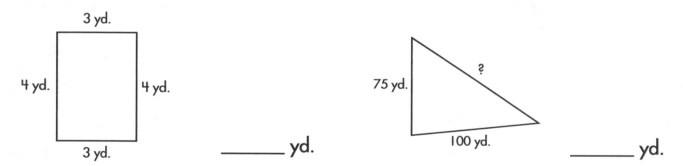

_____ yd.

_____ yd.

Jack made a rectangular play yard for his nephew. He tied a ribbon all the way around the outside for his nephew's birthday. Jack used 20 feet of ribbon. What is the perimeter of the play yard? Draw a picture and label the measurements of the play yard.

Lesson 5.9   Time

 5:15 is read "five fifteen" and means "15 minutes after 5."

 12:50 is read "twelve fifty" and means "50 minutes after 12" or "10 minutes to 1."

4:45 is read "four forty-five" and means "45 minutes after 4" or "15 minutes to 5."

Draw the hands on the analog clock and write the time in the digital clock to show the time described.

one ten

seven fifty-five

Laura leaves for work at 8:05 A.M. She drives for 40 minutes. What time does she get to work?

Laura has one hour for lunch. She leaves work at 12:00 P.M. and drives for 15 minutes to a restaurant. She spends 30 minutes eating lunch. Then, she drives for 15 minutes back to work. What time does she get back to work?

Lesson 5.10 Time on a Number Line

Carrie's family leaves home at 7:15 P.M. They stop at 8:30 P.M. for dinner. How long have they been driving?

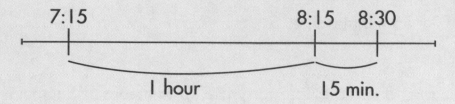

Carrie's family has been driving for 1 hour and 15 minutes.

Solve the problems. Use a number line to show your work.

Bonnie volunteers at an animal shelter and must be there at 1:00 P.M. She leaves the shelter at 4:30 P.M. and walks to her friend's house to eat dinner. She leaves her friend's house at 7:15 P.M. How much total time does Bonnie spend volunteering, walking, and eating dinner?

Perry parks his car at 6:57 P.M. He wants to visit the bookstore, so he puts enough money in the parking meter for 1 hour and 25 minutes. What time should Perry be back at his car?

Check What You Learned

Measurement

1. Mr. Daniels digs a vegetable garden that is 9 meters long by 7 meters wide. Draw a picture with unit squares to show the area of Mr. Daniels's vegetable garden.

$$A = \text{_____} \text{ sq. m}$$

2. Mr. Daniels wants to put a fence around his garden to keep the deer out. Find the perimeter of the garden to determine how much fencing Mr. Daniels needs to buy.

3. A farmer donated a plot of his land to the city. The plot of land was 20 kilometers by 3 kilometers. Some of the land will be turned into a city park. Another 9 kilometers by 3 kilometers is protected woods. Another 4 kilometers by 3 kilometers is swampland. How many kilometers of land will be turned into a city park?

Check What You Learned

Measurement

Delaney did some spring-cleaning at her house. She packed up all of her old clothes in plastic bags and took them to the donation center. She started cleaning her house at 8:30 A.M. and left to donate her clothes at 12:45 P.M.

4. Delaney used 4 9-gallon plastic bags to pack up her clothes. How many "gallons" of clothes did Delaney pack up?

5. Show on a number line how long Delaney was cleaning her house.

Complete the graphs.

6.

Miles Hiked
Amy = 20
Dustin = 5
Garrett = 10

Miles Hiked	

Key _____ = 5 miles

7.

Favorite Books
Fiction = 6
Nonfiction = 9
Poetry = 2

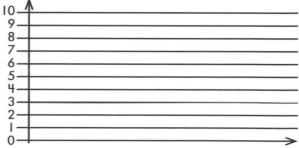

Favorite Books

Check What You Know

Geometry

1. Explain the difference between a square and a rectangle.

_____

_____

2. Explain the difference between a cube and a square pyramid.

_____

_____

3. Circle all of the quadrilaterals. Tell why the ones you did not circle are not quadrilaterals.

_____

_____

4. Banks orders a pizza from his favorite pizza place. When the pizza arrives, it is not cut into slices. Banks has invited over 5 of his friends. What fraction of the pizza will each person get if it is cut in equal slices?

5. Draw two pictures to show how to cut the pizza if it is in the shape of a circle and the shape of a rectangle.

Lesson 6.1 Plane Figures

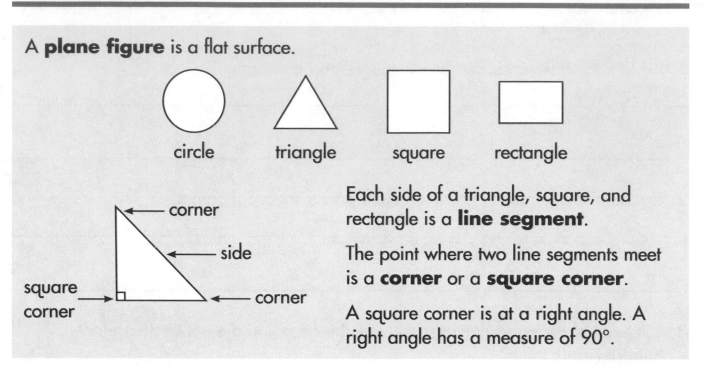

A **plane figure** is a flat surface.

circle   triangle   square   rectangle

corner
side
square corner → corner

Each side of a triangle, square, and rectangle is a **line segment**.

The point where two line segments meet is a **corner** or a **square corner**.

A square corner is at a right angle. A right angle has a measure of 90°.

Complete the chart.

	○	▭	△	⬠	⬡
# of sides					
# of square corners					
# of other corners					

Draw a real-world example of two of the shapes above.

Lesson 6.1   Plane Figures

You can write shape number sentences using shapes and numbers.

A triangle has 3 sides.
3 + 2 = 5
A shape that has five sides is a pentagon.

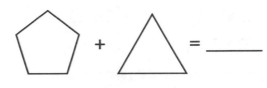

Solve the following shape number sentences.

Create 2 shape number sentences using the shapes below.

Lesson 6.2 Solid Figures

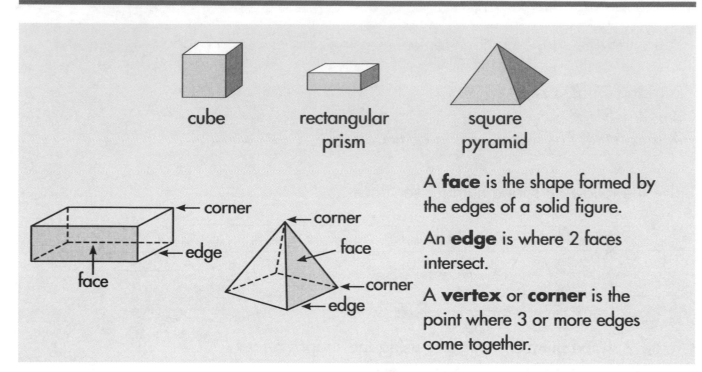

A **face** is the shape formed by the edges of a solid figure.

An **edge** is where 2 faces intersect.

A **vertex** or **corner** is the point where 3 or more edges come together.

Complete the table.

	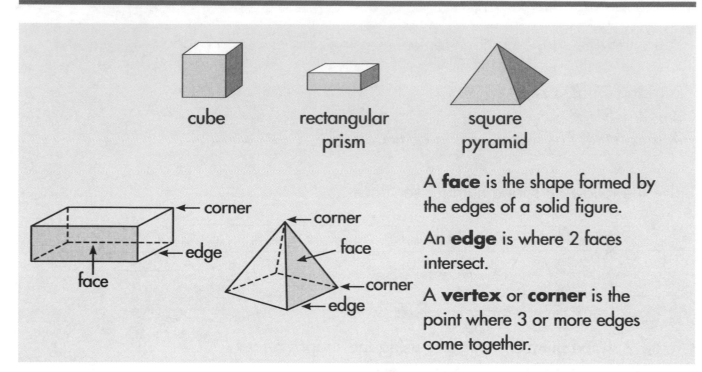		
# of faces			
# of edges			
# of vertices			

Lesson 6.2 Solid Figures

A baseball is a real-world
example of a sphere.

Write the name of the solid figure that each object represents.

Draw another real-world object that represents a solid shape you have learned about.

Lesson 6.3   Classifying Quadrilaterals

A trapezoid is a quadrilateral because it has 4 sides. A trapezoid is not a parallelogram because it does not have opposite sides parallel.

A **quadrilateral** is a polygon with 4 sides. Here are some examples:

parallelogram – a quadrilateral with opposite sides parallel

square – rectangle with 4 sides of the same length and all angles equal

rectangle – parallelogram with 4 right angles. Opposite sides are equal.

rhombus – parallelogram with all 4 sides the same length. Opposite angles are the same measure.

kite – 2 pairs of adjacent sides that are congruent

trapezoid – only 2 sides are parallel

Explain how a square can be a quadrilateral, a parallelogram, a rhombus, and a rectangle.

Explain how a rectangle is a quadrilateral and a parallelogram.

Lesson 6.4 Dividing Shapes

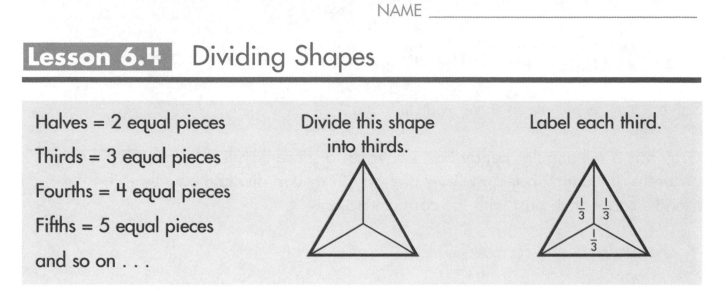

Halves = 2 equal pieces

Thirds = 3 equal pieces

Fourths = 4 equal pieces

Fifths = 5 equal pieces

and so on . . .

Divide this shape into thirds.

Label each third.

Answer the questions. Draw pictures to show each answer.

Benjamin is having some friends over for a dinner party. He is having a small rectangle-shaped cake for dessert. He is not sure if one of his 3 friends is going to make it to the dinner party. If all of Benjamin's friends come to the party, how should Benjamin cut the cake so he and his friends can each have an equal piece? If one of the friends does not make it, how should Benjamin cut the cake so he and his friends can each have an equal piece?

Mischa bought a large round cheese pizza to share with her family. There are 5 people in her family. Show how Mischa should cut the pizza so that everyone can have one equal piece. Then, show how Mischa should cut the pizza so that everyone can have one equal piece and there is one piece left over.

Lesson 6.5   Dividing Shapes in the Real World

Solve. Draw a picture to show your thinking.

Grey has a rectangular candy bar. He wants to share it with 3 friends. Draw a picture of the candy bar and show one way Grey can divide it equally with his friends. Label each part with the correct fraction.

Show another way Grey can divide the same candy bar, and label it.

Yolanda is planting a vegetable garden in a square-shaped bed. She wants to plant corn, peppers, squash, and lettuce. She must give each vegetable an equal amount of space in the garden. Draw a diagram that shows how Yolanda's garden can be divided so that all the vegetables get an equal amount of space. Is there another way to divide up the garden? If so, draw and label it.

Check What You Learned

Geometry

1. Mandy and her sister bake a cake to share with their grandmother for her birthday. When Mandy's grandmother first cuts the cake, it is only the 3 of them at her house. However, Grandmother's 3 neighbors come over and would like some cake, too. How can Mandy's grandmother cut the cake now so everyone can have a piece? Draw a picture to show your answer.

2. Name the shape that has the following:
   • zero sides
   • zero corners

   _____

3. Name the shape that has the following:
   • 1 square face
   • 4 triangle faces
   • 0 rectangle faces
   • 8 edges

   _____

4. Circle all the parallelograms. Then, tell why the ones you did not circle are not parallelograms.

   _____

   _____

Final Test Chapters 1–6

Solve the problems. Show your work.

1. There are 983 people who want tickets to a concert. There are 795 tickets available to purchase online. Local radio stations have 75 tickets to give away. How many people will not be able to get tickets?

2. The first 175 people who arrive at the concert will get a free T-shirt. If everyone who wins a ticket from a local radio station will get a free T-shirt, how many people who bought tickets online will get a free T-shirt?

3. Mr. King has 372 books in his classroom library. Ms. Lewis has 489 books in her classroom library. About how many books do Mr. King and Ms. Lewis have altogether?

4. About how many more books does Ms. Lewis have than Mr. King?

5. Both teachers are allowed to have 500 books in their classroom libraries. Exactly how many more books can each teacher have? Show your work.

Final Test   Chapters 1–6

Solve the problems. Show your work.

6. Sandra made 4 scarves with 32 feet of fabric. How many feet of fabric would Sandra need to make 35 scarves?

7. April has 12 scarves in her closet. 3 of the scarves are purple, 5 of the scarves are green, and the rest of the scarves have a pattern on them. How many of April's scarves have a pattern on them? Write a fraction for the purple scarves.

8. Over 10 days, Forrest earns $6 each day for doing household chores. Each day, his mom takes out $3 and puts it into a savings account for Forrest. How much total money does Forrest get to keep?

9. Brian has 63 candies. He wants to put the candy equally into 9 bags. How many candies does Brian need to put in each bag?

Final Test Chapters 1–6

10. Charlotte bakes 4 coconut cream pies for the bake sale. Norman bakes 4 banana cream pies for the bake sale. Each pie is cut into eighths, and each slice is sold individually. Write a fraction to show the pies Charlotte brings to the bake sale.

11. Write a fraction to show the amount of pie that Charlotte and Norman each made.

12. Each slice of pie was sold for $2. What was the total cost of a whole pie? Show your work.

13. Show the fraction $\frac{2}{8}$ in three different ways: on a number line, as part of a whole, and as part of a set.

Final Test Chapters 1–6

14. Casey plants a vegetable garden that is 8 meters long by 4 meters wide. Draw a picture and find the area of Casey's vegetable garden.

8

4

✓

32 sq. m

15. In the vegetable garden, Casey grows tomatoes, cucumbers, onions, peppers, and squash. By the end of the summer, he has harvested 15 cucumbers, 20 tomatoes, 5 onions, 10 peppers, and 15 squash. Draw a bar graph to show all the vegetables that Casey has harvested.

✓

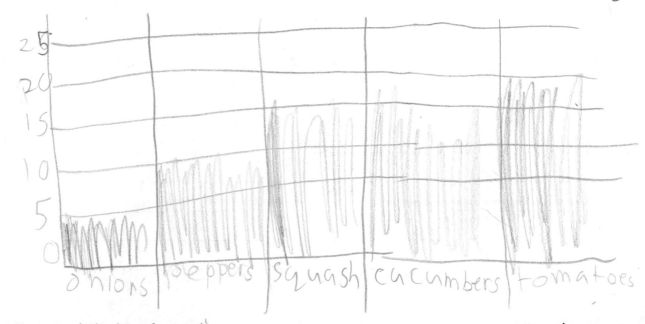

Spectrum Critical Thinking for Math
Grade 3

Final Test   Chapters 1–6

16. Roxanne wants to put a concrete patio behind her house. She wants it to look like the image shown below. The concrete company needs to know the area of the space where she wants her patio so they know how much concrete to pour. Find the area of the space.

18 sqf ✓

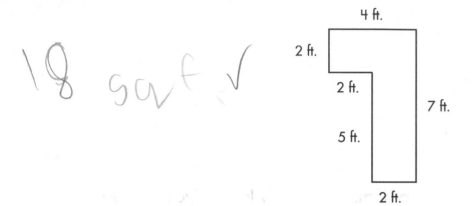

4 ft.

2 ft.

2 ft.

7 ft.

5 ft.

2 ft.

17. Roxanne also wants to put a special trim around the outside edge of the patio. Find the perimeter of the space to determine how much trim Roxanne will need.

22 ft ✓

18. Holly says a baby weighs 8 pounds. Kelsey says a baby weighs 8 ounces. Who is correct? Explain your thinking.

Holly because 8 ounces is too light for a baby. ✓

Spectrum Critical Thinking for Math
Grade 3
100

Chapters 1–6
Final Test

CHAPTERS 1–6 FINAL TEST

Final Test Chapters 1–6

Wyatt tries to drink a lot of water every day. He starts drinking water at 8:30 A.M. every morning, and stops drinking at 8:45 P.M. every evening.

19. Wyatt drinks 36 ounces before noon, and 36 ounces after noon. How many ounces does Wyatt drink altogether?

72 ounces ✓

20. Show on a number line how long Wyatt drinks water every day.

30 min   12 hrs   45 mins

8:30   9:00   8:00   8:45

12 hrs 15 mins

21. The following chart shows how many total ounces of water Wyatt drank over the past 3 days. Draw a picture graph to show the information in the chart.

water dank

Water (Ounces)	
Day 1	70
Day 2	80
Day 3	65

Key = ⬡ = 10 ounces

Spectrum Critical Thinking for Math
Grade 3

Chapters 1–6
Final Test
101

CHAPTERS 1–6 FINAL TEST

Final Test Chapters 1–6

22. As a treat, Ms. Rizzo makes a giant cookie shaped like a triangle. She divides her students into 3 groups with 2 people in each group. Then, she cuts the cookie into 3 pieces. She gives each group a piece. Ms. Rizzo tells each group they need to divide their piece so that each person gets a piece. Draw a picture to show how Ms. Rizzo divided the giant triangle cookie for the whole club. Then draw a picture to show how each group divided their cookie.

23. Brad tells Shelby that a trapezoid is a parallelogram, but not a quadrilateral. Shelby is unsure. Is Brad right? Explain your answer.

No because a parallelogram has to have to
have 2 pairs of parallel sides. A trapezoid
and a parallelogram are quadrilateral

24. Name both figures shown. Explain how they are the same and how they are different.

Circle and sphere. They both don't have
vertices. The circle is fat butt the
sphere is not

Emma werthon

Answer Key

Page 4

NAME _____

CHAPTER 1 PRETEST

Check What You Know

Adding and Subtracting Through 2-Digit Numbers

Solve for each unknown. Write the addition or subtraction sentence you used to solve. Show your work.

1. Bailey needs to read 75 pages by the day after tomorrow. She read some pages today and has 30 pages left. How many pages did Bailey read today?

$$75 - 30 = 45$$

2. Ivan is going to visit his aunt. He travels 32 miles on Saturday. He travels 15 miles farther on Sunday than he did on Saturday. How many miles did Ivan travel on Sunday?

$$32 + 15 = 47$$

3. The Murphy Library has 52 computers. It has 29 desktop computers, and the rest are laptop computers. How many laptops does the library have?

$$52 - 29 = 23$$

Spectrum Critical Thinking for Math
Grade 3
4

Chapter 1
Check What You Know

Page 5

NAME _____

Lesson 1.1 Finding Unknowns

You can find unknown numbers in an addition sentence by subtracting the given numbers.

$? + 19 = 52$

Begin with the sum and subtract the addend you are given.

Rename 52 as "4 tens and 12 ones."	Subtract the ones.	Subtract the tens.
$\begin{array}{r} 52 \\ -19 \\ \hline \end{array}$ $\begin{array}{r} {}^{4\ 12} \\ 5\!\!\!/2 \\ -19 \\ \hline \end{array}$	$\begin{array}{r} {}^{4\ 12} \\ 5\!\!\!/2 \\ -19 \\ \hline 3 \end{array}$	$\begin{array}{r} {}^{4\ 12} \\ 5\!\!\!/2 \\ -19 \\ \hline 33 \end{array}$ minuend subtrahend difference

Subtract to find the missing addends. Show your work.

After the family reunion, Javier washed 25 plates by hand in the sink. He also washed some cups. When Javier finished, he had washed 51 dishes. How many cups did Javier wash?

$$\begin{array}{r} {}^{4\ 11} \\ 5\!\!\!/1 \\ -25 \\ \hline 26 \end{array}$$

Javier washed 26 cups.

Of the 25 plates Javier washed, some were plastic and some were not. If 15 of the plates were plastic, how many were not plastic?

$$\begin{array}{r} 25 \\ -15 \\ \hline 10 \end{array}$$

10 of the plates were not plastic.

Spectrum Critical Thinking for Math
Grade 3

Lesson 1.1
Finding Unknowns
5

Page 6

NAME _____

Lesson 1.1 Finding Unknowns

You can use a number line to find unknown addends in an addition problem.

$48 + ? = 64$

Begin your number line on the right side with the sum. Using tens and ones, count backward to the amount of the given addend.

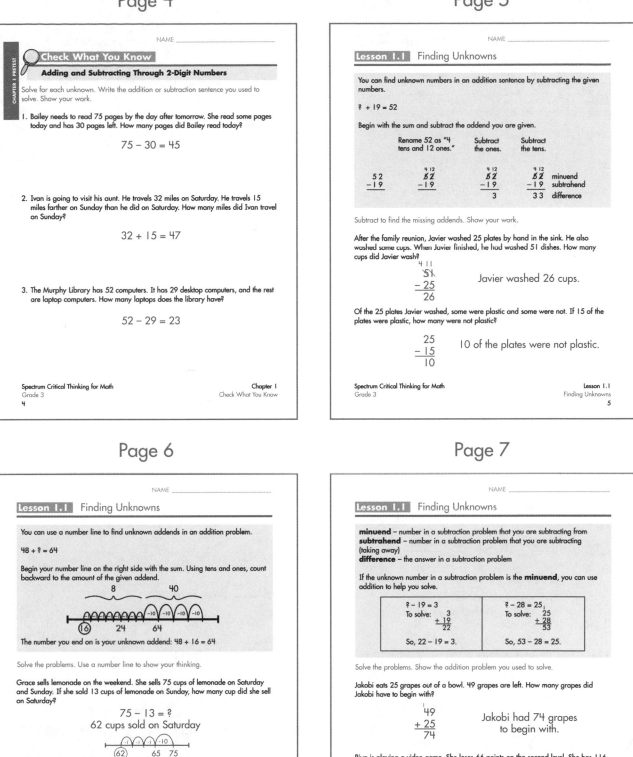

The number you end on is your unknown addend: $48 + 16 = 64$

Solve the problems. Use a number line to show your thinking.

Grace sells lemonade on the weekend. She sells 75 cups of lemonade on Saturday and Sunday. If she sold 13 cups of lemonade on Sunday, how many cup did she sell on Saturday?

$$75 - 13 = ?$$
62 cups sold on Saturday

Grace bought 36 lemons to make the lemonade. She used 23 lemons for Saturday's lemonade. How many lemons did she have left for Sunday's lemonade?

$$36 - 23 = ?$$
13 lemons left for Sunday

Spectrum Critical Thinking for Math
Grade 3
6

Lesson 1.1
Finding Unknowns

Page 7

NAME _____

Lesson 1.1 Finding Unknowns

minuend – number in a subtraction problem that you are subtracting from
subtrahend – number in a subtraction problem that you are subtracting (taking away)
difference – the answer in a subtraction problem

If the unknown number in a subtraction problem is the **minuend**, you can use addition to help you solve.

$? - 19 = 3$ To solve: $\begin{array}{r} 3 \\ +19 \\ \hline 22 \end{array}$	$? - 28 = 25$ To solve: $\begin{array}{r} 25 \\ +28 \\ \hline 53 \end{array}$
So, $22 - 19 = 3$.	So, $53 - 28 = 25$.

Solve the problems. Show the addition problem you used to solve.

Jakobi eats 25 grapes out of a bowl. 49 grapes are left. How many grapes did Jakobi have to begin with?

$$\begin{array}{r} 49 \\ +25 \\ \hline 74 \end{array}$$

Jakobi had 74 grapes to begin with.

Riya is playing a video game. She loses 66 points on the second level. She has 116 points left. How many points did she start the second level with?

$$\begin{array}{r} 116 \\ +66 \\ \hline 182 \end{array}$$

Riya started the second level with 182 points.

Spectrum Critical Thinking for Math
Grade 3

Lesson 1.1
Finding Unknowns
7

Answer Key

Page 8

NAME _____

Lesson 1.1 Finding Unknowns

Solve each problem. Show the addition problem you used to solve.

John has a jar of candy. He shares the candy with his book club group and they eat 62 pieces of the candy. Now, there are 127 pieces of candy left in John's jar. How many pieces of candy were in John's jar to start with?

$$\begin{array}{r} 127 \\ + 62 \\ \hline 189 \end{array}$$ There were 189 pieces to start with.

In her gymnastics competition, Hannah earned points for every event she competed in. However, the judges took away points as well. The judges took 41 points away from Hannah's total score. Hannah's final score was 92 points. How many points did Hannah earn before points were taken away?

$$\begin{array}{r} 41 \\ + 92 \\ \hline 133 \end{array}$$ Hannah earned 133 points before some were taken away.

Hannah's teammates scored 439 points in the gymnastics competition. How many total points did the team score?

$$\begin{array}{r} 439 \\ + 92 \\ \hline 531 \end{array}$$ The team scored 531 total points.

Spectrum Critical Thinking for Math
Grade 3
8

Lesson 1.1
Finding Unknowns

Page 9

NAME _____

Lesson 1.1 Finding Unknowns

If the unknown number in a subtraction problem is the **subtrahend**, you can use subtraction to help you solve.

$83 - ? = 17$

Subtract the smaller number from the larger number.

$$\begin{array}{r} 83 \\ - 17 \\ \hline 66 \end{array}$$

$83 - 17 = 66$. So, $83 - 66 = 17$.

Solve the problems. Write the subtraction problem you used to solve and show your work.

Cindy had 34 tins of popcorn to sell. After a day of walking around her neighborhood and selling popcorn to all of her neighbors, she has 19 tins of popcorn left. How many tins of popcorn did Cindy sell?

$$\begin{array}{r} 34 \\ - 19 \\ \hline 15 \end{array}$$ Cindy sold 15 tins.

If 12 of the remaining tins are filled with caramel popcorn, and the rest are butter, how many tins are butter popcorn?

$$\begin{array}{r} 19 \\ - 12 \\ \hline 7 \end{array}$$ 7 tins are butter popcorn.

Spectrum Critical Thinking for Math
Grade 3

Lesson 1.1
Finding Unknowns
9

Page 10

NAME _____

Lesson 1.4 Adding and Subtracting in the Real World

Solve the problems. Show your work.

Brenda has a jar of gumballs. In the jar are 42 red gumballs and 27 yellow gumballs.

What is the total number of gumballs in the jar?

$$\begin{array}{r} 42 \\ + 27 \\ \hline 69 \end{array}$$ There are 69 total gumballs in the jar.

If Brenda removes 23 gumballs from the jar, how many will she have left? What is one possible combination of red and yellow gumballs left?

$$\begin{array}{r} 69 \\ - 23 \\ \hline 46 \end{array}$$ There will be 46 gumballs left.

Answers will vary.

After removing 23 gumballs from the jar, Brenda adds 12 purple gumballs and 33 green gumballs. How many total gumballs are in the jar now?

$$\begin{array}{r} 46 \\ 12 \\ + 33 \\ \hline 91 \end{array}$$ There are now 91 total gumballs in the jar.

Spectrum Critical Thinking for Math
Grade 3
10

Lesson 1.4
Adding and Subtracting in the Real World

Page 11

NAME _____

Lesson 1.2 Checking Answers

You can use opposite operations to check the answer to an addition or subtraction problem.

Addition: $45 + 12 = 57$
Check using subtraction: $57 - 12 = 45$, and $57 - 45 = 12$

Subtraction: $69 - 12 = 57$
Check using addition: $57 + 12 = 69$

Check each problem using opposite operations. Tell if the answer is correct. If it is not, give the correct answer. Show your work.

Anabel buys 15 tomato plants and 22 pepper plants. She thinks she has $15 + 22 = 38$ total plants. Is she correct?

$$\begin{array}{r} 38 \\ - 15 \\ \hline 23 \end{array}$$ No, she is not correct.
She has $15 + 22 = 37$ plants.

Mykal and Lin bought 68 party invitations and mailed out 46 of them. Lin says they have $68 - 46 = 22$ invitations left. Is he correct?

$$\begin{array}{r} 46 \\ + 22 \\ \hline 68 \end{array}$$ Yes, he is correct.

Spectrum Critical Thinking for Math
Grade 3

Lesson 1.2
Checking Answers
11

Answer Key

Page 12

NAME _____

Lesson 1.3 Opposite Operations on a Number Line

You can write a number sentence based on a completed number line.

154 – 13 = 141

The addition sentence is the opposite.

141 + 13 = 154

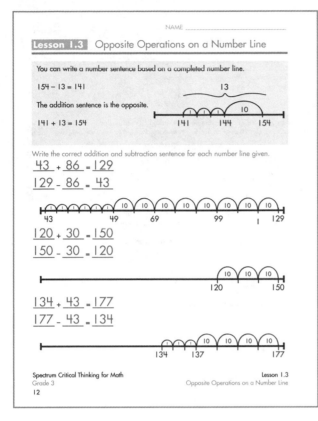

Write the correct addition and subtraction sentence for each number line given.

43 + 86 = 129
129 – 86 = 43

120 + 30 = 150
150 – 30 = 120

134 + 43 = 177
177 – 43 = 134

Spectrum Critical Thinking for Math
Grade 3
12

Lesson 1.3
Opposite Operations on a Number Line

Page 13

NAME _____

Lesson 1.4 Adding 3 Numbers

6 + 13 + 29 = ?
Begin with the first addend, 6. Count forward by tens and ones until you count your second addend. Write the number.
Then, count forward by tens and ones until you count your third addend. Write the number. The number you stop at is your answer.

Solve each problem. Use a number line to show your thinking.

Mr. Dolby has 15 students in his class. Ms. Avila has 30 students in her class. Ms. Schmidt has 28 students in her class. How many total students are in the 3 classes?

15 + 30 + 28 = ?
73 total students

In Mr. Dolby's class, 13 students turned in their homework. In Ms. Avila's class, 18 students turned in their homework. In Ms. Schmidt's class, 17 students turned in their homework. How many total students turned in their homework?

13 + 18 + 17 = ?
48 total students

Spectrum Critical Thinking for Math
Grade 3

Lesson 1.4
Adding 3 Numbers
13

Page 14

NAME _____

Lesson 1.5 Adding 3 Numbers in the Real World

Read each problem and solve. Write the addition sentence you used to solve and show your work under each question.

Marisa's school is holding a fall festival to raise money. Students can play games to collect points and win prizes. The table below shows which prizes students can claim and how many points are needed for each prize.

Prize	Points
necklace	11
hat	35
stuffed animal	39
sticker book	27
fish	42

Marisa's goal is to collect a necklace, a fish, and a stuffed animal. How many points does she have to earn?

```
  11
  42
+ 39
────
  92
```

Marisa needs to earn 92 points to collect a necklace, a fish, and a stuffed animal.

Marisa's little brother has earned 98 points. What are 2 combinations of 3 prizes that he can choose?

Answers will vary. Possible answers:

necklace, hat, stuffed animal: fish, necklace, sticker book:

11 + 35 + 39 = 85   42 + 11 + 27 = 80

Spectrum Critical Thinking for Math
Grade 3
14

Lesson 1.5
Adding 3 Numbers in the Real World

Page 15

NAME _____

Lesson 1.6 Unknowns in 3-Number Problems

To find an unknown addend in a 3-number addition problem, you must complete 2 steps of adding and subtracting to find your answer.

13 + ? + 45 = 84

First, add together the addends you are given: 13 + 45 = 58

Then, subtract that sum from the total given:
```
  7 14
  8̶4̶
– 58
────
  26
```

The answer you get is the unknown addend: 13 + 26 + 45 = 84

Solve each problem. Write the addition and subtraction problem you use. Show your work.

Jimmy has 64 square buttons in his button collection. Some of them are blue, 23 of them are red, and 25 of them are green. How many of Jimmy's square buttons are blue?

```
  23        5 14
+ 25        6̶4̶
────      – 48
  48      ────
            16
```

Jimmy has 16 square buttons.

Jimmy also has buttons with other shapes. He has 45 oval buttons, 32 triangle buttons, and some buttons shaped like flowers. The total number of oval, triangle, and flower buttons is 107. How many buttons are shaped like flowers?

```
  45        0 10
+ 32        1̶0̶7̶
────      – 77
  77      ────
            30
```

Jimmy has 30 buttons shaped like flowers.

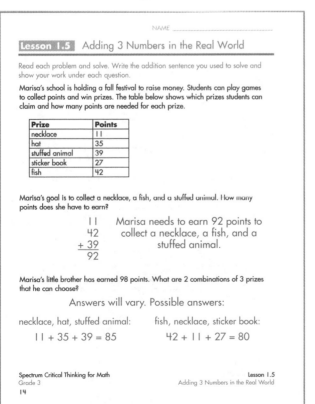
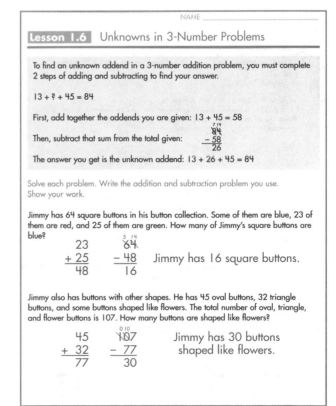

105

Answer Key

Page 16

NAME _____

Lesson 1.7 Find the Unknown and Check the Answer

Alicia has 52 ice pops. She has 23 apple ice pops, some grape ice pops, and 11 cherry ice pops. How many grape ice pops does she have?

23 + ? + 11 = 52
23 + 11 = 34; 52 − 34 = 18; 23 + 18 + 11 = 52
18 of the ice pops are grape.

Now, check your answer with a number line.
Begin with 23. Count forward by tens and ones until you count the second addend. Write the number. Then, count forward by tens and ones until you count the third addend. Write the number. The number you stop at is the answer.

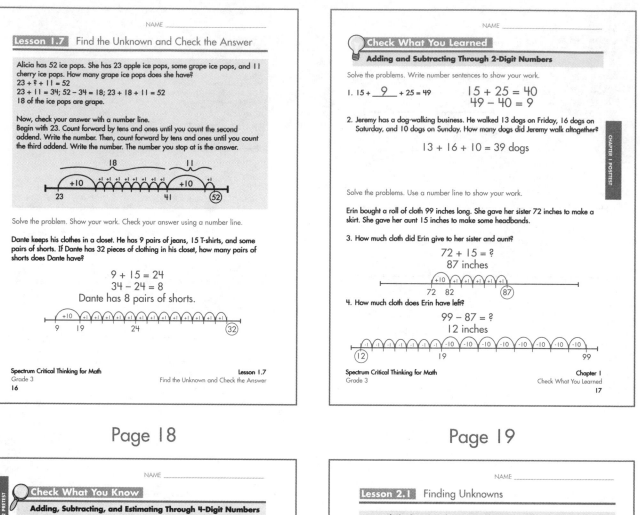

Solve the problem. Show your work. Check your answer using a number line.

Dante keeps his clothes in a closet. He has 9 pairs of jeans, 15 T-shirts, and some pairs of shorts. If Dante has 32 pieces of clothing in his closet, how many pairs of shorts does Dante have?

9 + 15 = 24
34 − 24 = 8
Dante has 8 pairs of shorts.

Spectrum Critical Thinking for Math
Grade 3
16

Lesson 1.7
Find the Unknown and Check the Answer

Page 17

NAME _____

Check What You Learned
Adding and Subtracting Through 2-Digit Numbers

Solve the problems. Write number sentences to show your work.

1. 15 + _9_ + 25 = 49   15 + 25 = 40
                           49 − 40 = 9

2. Jeremy has a dog-walking business. He walked 13 dogs on Friday, 16 dogs on Saturday, and 10 dogs on Sunday. How many dogs did Jeremy walk altogether?

13 + 16 + 10 = 39 dogs

Solve the problems. Use a number line to show your work.

Erin bought a roll of cloth 99 inches long. She gave her sister 72 inches to make a skirt. She gave her aunt 15 inches to make some headbands.

3. How much cloth did Erin give to her sister and aunt?

72 + 15 = ?
87 inches

4. How much cloth does Erin have left?

99 − 87 = ?
12 inches

Spectrum Critical Thinking for Math
Grade 3

Chapter 1
Check What You Learned
17

Page 18

NAME _____

Check What You Know
Adding, Subtracting, and Estimating Through 4-Digit Numbers

Solve. Show your work.

1. Lee Elementary School has 1,695 students. Davidson Elementary School has 1,523 students. At the beginning of every year, each student is given a student planner. About how many planners are needed at Lee Elementary School? About how many are needed at Davidson Elementary School?

About 1,700 planners are needed at
Lee Elementary School.

About 1,500 planners are needed at
Davidson Elementary School.

2. If both schools buy 2,000 planners each, will they have enough planners to give 1 to each child?

```
 1700      2000
+ 1500    + 2000
 3,200     4,000
```

The schools need a total of about 3,200 planners. So yes, they will have enough.

3. Exactly how many planners will be left over after each student is given 1?

```
 1695      4000
+ 1523    − 3218
 3,218      782
```

There will be 782 planners left over.

Spectrum Critical Thinking for Math
Grade 3
18

Chapter 2
Check What You Know

Page 19

NAME _____

Lesson 2.1 Finding Unknowns

You can find unknown numbers in an addition sentence by subtracting the given numbers.

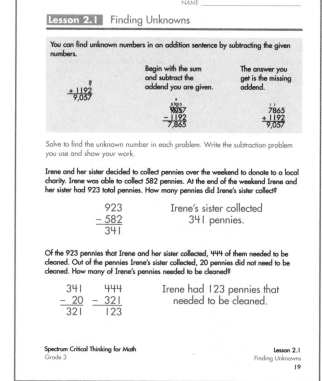

Begin with the sum and subtract the addend you are given.

The answer you get is the missing addend.

```
    ?
+ 1192
 9,057
```

```
  8 10 15
  9 0 5 7
 − 1 1 9 2
  7,865
```

```
    1 1
   7865
 + 1192
  9,057
```

Solve to find the unknown number in each problem. Write the subtraction problem you use and show your work.

Irene and her sister decided to collect pennies over the weekend to donate to a local charity. Irene was able to collect 582 pennies. At the end of the weekend Irene and her sister had 923 total pennies. How many pennies did Irene's sister collect?

```
  923
− 582
  341
```

Irene's sister collected
341 pennies.

Of the 923 pennies that Irene and her sister collected, 444 of them needed to be cleaned. Out of the pennies Irene's sister collected, 20 pennies did not need to be cleaned. How many of Irene's pennies needed to be cleaned?

```
 341      444
−  20    − 321
 321      123
```

Irene had 123 pennies that needed to be cleaned.

Spectrum Critical Thinking for Math
Grade 3

Lesson 2.1
Finding Unknowns
19

Answer Key

Page 20

NAME _____

Lesson 2.1 Finding Unknowns

Find the unknown number in each problem. Write the subtraction problem you use and show your work.

<u>6,216</u> + 1,219 = 7,435

$$\begin{array}{r} {\scriptstyle 2\ 15} \\ 74\cancel{3}5 \\ -\ 1219 \\ \hline 6,216 \end{array}$$

Kayla and Lamar are selling bracelets. So far, they have sold 1,255 blue bracelets, and some red bracelets. They have made some money from selling the blue bracelets and $5,028 from selling the red bracelets.

How many red bracelets have Kayla and Lamar sold so far if the total number of bracelets they sold was 3,769?

$$\begin{array}{r} 3769 \\ -\ 1255 \\ \hline 2,514 \end{array}$$

Kayla and Lamar have sold 2,514 red bracelets so far.

How much money have Kayla and Lamar made from selling blue bracelets if their total income so far is $7,538?

$$\begin{array}{r} \$7538 \\ -\ \$5028 \\ \hline \$2,510 \end{array}$$

Kayla and Lamar have made $2,510 from selling the blue bracelets so far.

Spectrum Critical Thinking for Math
Grade 3
20

Lesson 2.1
Finding Unknowns

Page 21

NAME _____

Lesson 2.1 Finding Unknowns

You can find unknown numbers in an addition sentence by subtracting the given numbers on a number line: 7,986 + ? = 9,232

Start with the larger number at the right of the number line. Subtract by 1000s, 100s, 10s, and 1s until you reach the smaller number. Add together the 1000s, 100s, 10s, and 1s you subtracted to get the unknown addend.

1,246

7,986   7,992   8,032   8,232   9,232

7,986 + 1,246 = 9,232

Find the missing addends. Show your work using subtraction on a number line.

The booster club sells raffle tickets at school events. At Saturday's soccer game, the booster club sold 681 total raffle tickets. 431 of those tickets were sold at the gate. The rest were sold at halftime. How many tickets were sold at halftime?

431 + 250 = 681
250 tickets were sold at halftime.

At the school musical, the booster club sold 314 fewer total tickets than it did at the soccer game. It sold 175 tickets at the door and the rest at the snack bar. How many tickets did the booster club sell at the snack bar?

681 – 314 = 367
175 + 192 = 367
The booster club sold 192 tickets at the snack bar.

Spectrum Critical Thinking for Math
Grade 3
21

Lesson 2.1
Finding Unknowns

Page 22

NAME _____

Lesson 2.1 Finding Unknowns

Find each unknown. Show your work on a number line.

<u>203</u> + 211 = 414

414 – 211 = 203

Tickets went on sale for the soccer playoff game 2 weeks ago. The first week, 3,971 soccer tickets were sold. The second week, more tickets were sold. A total of 8,915 tickets were sold for the playoff game. How many tickets were sold the second week?

8,915 – 3,971 = 4,944

4,944 tickets were sold the second week.

Of the 8,915 tickets sold, 4,502 were fans of the home team and the rest were fans of the visiting team. How many were fans of the visiting team?

8,915 – 4,502 = 4,413

4,413 were fans of the visiting team.

Spectrum Critical Thinking for Math
Grade 3
22

Lesson 2.1
Finding Unknowns

Page 23

NAME _____

Lesson 2.1 Finding Unknowns

If the unknown number in a subtraction problem is the minuend, you can use addition to help you solve: ? – 2,382 = 7,483

Start with the difference and add the subtrahend:

$$\begin{array}{r} {\scriptstyle 1} \\ 7483 \\ +\ 2382 \\ \hline 9,865 \end{array}$$

The answer you get for the addition problem is the unknown value:

$$\begin{array}{r} {\scriptstyle 7\ 16} \\ 9\cancel{8}\cancel{6}5 \\ -\ 2382 \\ \hline 7,483 \end{array}$$

Solve each problem. Write the addition problem you used to solve.

On Thursday, the milkshake shop served 721 milkshakes, which is 142 fewer than it served on Wednesday. How many milkshakes did it serve on Wednesday?

$$\begin{array}{r} ? \\ -\ 142 \\ \hline 721 \end{array} \qquad \begin{array}{r} 721 \\ +\ 142 \\ \hline 863 \end{array}$$

The shop served 863 milkshakes on Wednesday.

On the other five days of the week, the milkshake shop served a total of 3,237 milkshakes. How many milkshakes did it serve for the entire week?

$$\begin{array}{r} 721 \\ +\ 863 \\ \hline 1,584 \end{array} \qquad \begin{array}{r} ? \\ -\ 1584 \\ \hline 3,237 \end{array} \qquad \begin{array}{r} 3237 \\ +\ 1584 \\ \hline 4,821 \end{array}$$

The shop served 4,821 milkshakes for the entire week.

Spectrum Critical Thinking for Math
Grade 3
23

Lesson 2.1
Finding Unknowns

Answer Key

Page 24

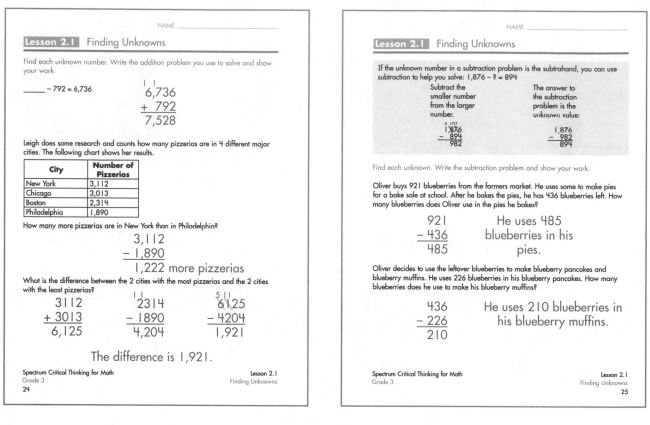

NAME _____

Lesson 2.1 Finding Unknowns

Find each unknown number. Write the addition problem you use to solve and show your work.

_____ − 792 = 6,736

$$\begin{array}{r} \overset{1\ 1}{6{,}736} \\ +\ \ \ 792 \\ \hline 7{,}528 \end{array}$$

Leigh does some research and counts how many pizzerias are in 4 different major cities. The following chart shows her results.

City	Number of Pizzerias
New York	3,112
Chicago	3,013
Boston	2,314
Philadelphia	1,890

How many more pizzerias are in New York than in Philadelphia?

$$\begin{array}{r} 3{,}112 \\ -\ 1{,}890 \\ \hline 1{,}222 \end{array} \text{ more pizzerias}$$

What is the difference between the 2 cities with the most pizzerias and the 2 cities with the least pizzerias?

$$\begin{array}{r} \overset{1\ 1}{3112} \\ +\ 3013 \\ \hline 6{,}125 \end{array} \qquad \begin{array}{r} \overset{1\ 1}{2314} \\ -\ 1890 \\ \hline 4{,}204 \end{array} \qquad \begin{array}{r} \overset{5\ 11}{6125} \\ -\ 4204 \\ \hline 1{,}921 \end{array}$$

The difference is 1,921.

Spectrum Critical Thinking for Math
Grade 3
24

Lesson 2.1
Finding Unknowns

Page 25

NAME _____

Lesson 2.1 Finding Unknowns

If the unknown number in a subtraction problem is the subtrahand, you can use subtraction to help you solve: 1,876 − ? = 894

Subtract the smaller number from the larger number.	The answer to the subtraction problem is the unknown value:
$\begin{array}{r} \overset{0\ 1717}{1{,}8\cancel{7}6} \\ -\ \ 894 \\ \hline 982 \end{array}$	$\begin{array}{r} 1{,}876 \\ -\ \ 982 \\ \hline 894 \end{array}$

Find each unknown. Write the subtraction problem and show your work.

Oliver buys 921 blueberries from the farmers market. He uses some to make pies for a bake sale at school. After he bakes the pies, he has 436 blueberries left. How many blueberries does Oliver use in the pies he bakes?

$$\begin{array}{r} 921 \\ -\ 436 \\ \hline 485 \end{array} \qquad \text{He uses 485 blueberries in his pies.}$$

Oliver decides to use the leftover blueberries to make blueberry pancakes and blueberry muffins. He uses 226 blueberries in his blueberry pancakes. How many blueberries does he use to make his blueberry muffins?

$$\begin{array}{r} 436 \\ -\ 226 \\ \hline 210 \end{array} \qquad \text{He uses 210 blueberries in his blueberry muffins.}$$

Spectrum Critical Thinking for Math
Grade 3

Lesson 2.1
Finding Unknowns
25

Page 26

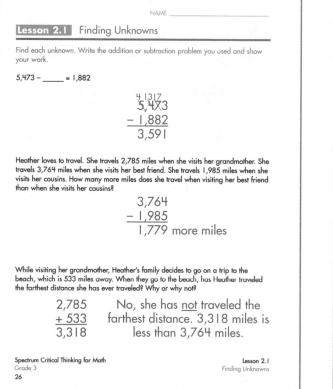

NAME _____

Lesson 2.1 Finding Unknowns

Find each unknown. Write the addition or subtraction problem you used and show your work.

5,473 − _____ = 1,882

$$\begin{array}{r} \overset{4\ 1317}{5{,}\cancel{4}\cancel{7}3} \\ -\ 1{,}882 \\ \hline 3{,}591 \end{array}$$

Heather loves to travel. She travels 2,785 miles when she visits her grandmother. She travels 3,764 miles when she visits her best friend. She travels 1,985 miles when she visits her cousins. How many more miles does she travel when visiting her best friend than when she visits her cousins?

$$\begin{array}{r} 3{,}764 \\ -\ 1{,}985 \\ \hline 1{,}779 \end{array} \text{ more miles}$$

While visiting her grandmother, Heather's family decides to go on a trip to the beach, which is 533 miles away. When they go to the beach, has Heather traveled the farthest distance she has ever traveled? Why or why not?

$$\begin{array}{r} 2{,}785 \\ +\ \ 533 \\ \hline 3{,}318 \end{array} \qquad \text{No, she has \underline{not} traveled the farthest distance. 3,318 miles is less than 3,764 miles.}$$

Spectrum Critical Thinking for Math
Grade 3
26

Lesson 2.1
Finding Unknowns

Page 27

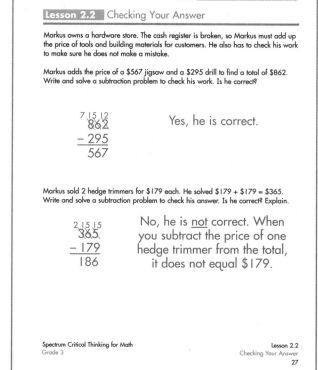

NAME _____

Lesson 2.2 Checking Your Answer

Markus owns a hardware store. The cash register is broken, so Markus must add up the price of tools and building materials for customers. He also has to check his work to make sure he does not make a mistake.

Markus adds the price of a $567 jigsaw and a $295 drill to find a total of $862. Write and solve a subtraction problem to check his work. Is he correct?

$$\begin{array}{r} \overset{7\ 15\ 12}{8\cancel{6}\cancel{2}} \\ -\ 295 \\ \hline 567 \end{array} \qquad \text{Yes, he is correct.}$$

Markus sold 2 hedge trimmers for $179 each. He solved $179 + $179 = $365. Write and solve a subtraction problem to check his answer. Is he correct? Explain.

$$\begin{array}{r} \overset{2\ 15\ 15}{3\cancel{6}\cancel{5}} \\ -\ 179 \\ \hline 186 \end{array} \qquad \text{No, he is \underline{not} correct. When you subtract the price of one hedge trimmer from the total, it does not equal \$179.}$$

Spectrum Critical Thinking for Math
Grade 3
27

Lesson 2.2
Checking Your Answer

Answer Key

Page 28

NAME

Lesson 2.2 Checking Your Answer

You can use opposite operations to check the answer to an addition or subtraction problem with larger numbers.

Addition: 466 + 435 = 901
Check using subtraction: 901 – 466 = 435, and 901 – 435 = 466

Subtraction: 801 – 148 = 653
Check using addition: 653 + 148 = 801

Check each problem using opposite operations. Tell if the answer is correct. If it is not, give the correct answer. Show your work.

Ms. Chan's class collected 323 cans of food for the school food drive. Mr. Okafor's class collected 345 cans. The students counted and said they had a total of 323 + 345 = 670 cans. Were they correct?

$$
\begin{array}{r}
6\ 10 \\
6\cancel{7}\cancel{0} \\
-\ 323 \\
\hline
347
\end{array}
$$

No, they were <u>not</u> correct. When you subtract the number of cans collected by Ms. Chan's class from the total, it does not equal 345.

Jessa saved $115 from her allowance and $160 from selling lemonade. She counted $115 + $160 = $275 that she could spend on a new computer. Was she correct?

$$
\begin{array}{r}
275 \\
-\ 115 \\
\hline
160
\end{array}
$$

Yes, she is correct.

Page 29

NAME

Lesson 2.3 Real-World Addition and Subtraction

Solve each problem. Show your work.

Nellie sells tickets to events at her school. So far, she has sold 321 adult tickets and 262 children's tickets for a walkathon. How many tickets has Nellie sold for the walkathon? How many more total tickets would Nellie have to sell to reach her goal of 700 tickets sold?

$$
\begin{array}{r}
321\ \text{adult} \\
+\ 262\ \text{children} \\
\hline
583\ \text{tickets}
\end{array}
\qquad
\begin{array}{r}
700 \\
-\ 583 \\
\hline
117\ \text{more}
\end{array}
$$

Andrew works at an ice cream shop. He made a chart that shows how many scoops of ice cream he sold each day from Monday to Friday.

Monday	118
Tuesday	105
Wednesday	345
Thursday	126
Friday	612

On the weekend, Andrew sold 980 scoops of ice cream. How many more scoops did Andrew sell on the weekend than he did on Thursday and Friday?

$$
\begin{array}{r}
126\ \text{Thursday} \\
+\ 612\ \text{Friday} \\
\hline
738
\end{array}
\qquad
\begin{array}{r}
980\ \text{weekend} \\
-\ 738\ \text{Thursday \& Friday} \\
\hline
242\ \text{more}
\end{array}
$$

Page 30

NAME

Lesson 2.3 Real-World Addition and Subtraction

Solve the problems. Write the addition and subtraction sentences you used to solve. Show your work.

Students in the math club are selling two types of calendars. So far, they have sold 1,327 farm animal calendars and 3,915 puppy calendars. The students have made $2,534 from selling the farm animal calendars and $4,699 from selling the puppy calendars. How many calendars have the students sold so far? How much money have the students made so far?

$$
\begin{array}{r}
1327\ \text{farm} \\
+\ 3915\ \text{puppy} \\
\hline
5,242\ \text{calendars}
\end{array}
\qquad
\begin{array}{r}
\$2534 \\
+\ \$4699 \\
\hline
\$7,233
\end{array}
$$

The students have sold 5,242 calendars so far and made $7,233.

The aquarium gift shop has a large collection of magnets. Dawson made the chart below to show how many magnets the gift shop has of several different animals.

Animal	Magnets
Dolphins	1,942
Sharks	6,413
Red Zebra Fish	4,120
Sea Turtles	2,817

How many more shark magnets does the gift shop have than sea turtle and dolphin magnets?

$$
\begin{array}{r}
2817\ \text{sea turtles} \\
+\ 1942\ \text{dolphins} \\
\hline
4,759
\end{array}
\qquad
\begin{array}{r}
6413\ \text{sharks} \\
-\ 4759\ \text{turtles and dolphins} \\
\hline
1,654
\end{array}
$$

The gift shop has 1,654 more shark magnets than sea turtle magnets and dolphin magnets.

Page 31

NAME

Lesson 2.4 Estimating Addition

You can use a number line to help you estimate addends in an addition problem.

Draw a number line and show the two closest tens to the addend.
Plot the number on the number line.
If the number is before the 5, it rounds down to the lower ten.
If the number is on or after the 5, it rounds up to the higher ten.

Add the rounded numbers together to get the estimated answer.

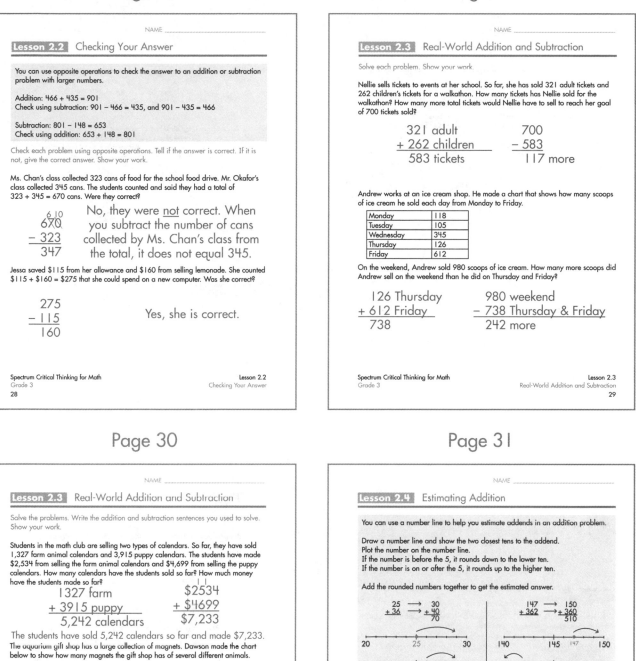

Use a number line to show how to round each addend to the nearest ten. Then, solve.

57 + 51 = 60 + 50 = 110

357 + 603 = 360 + 600 = 960

Answer Key

Page 32

NAME _____

Lesson 2.5 Estimating Subtraction

You can use a number line to help you estimate the minuend and subtrahend in a subtraction problem.

Draw a number line and show the two closest tens to the number.
Plot the number on the number line.
If the number is before the 5, it rounds down to the lower ten.
If the number is on or after the 5, it rounds up to the higher ten.

Subtract the rounded numbers to get your answer.

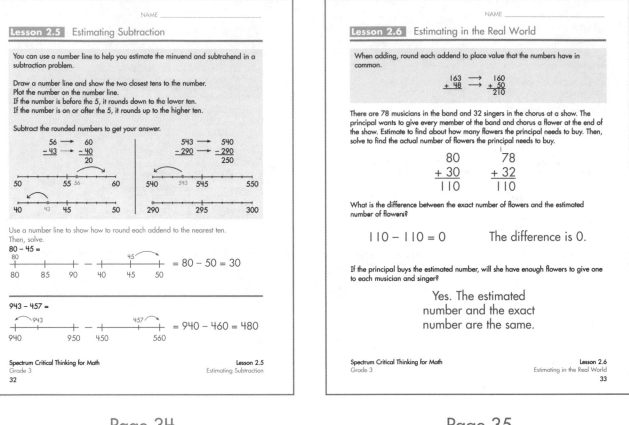

Use a number line to show how to round each addend to the nearest ten. Then, solve.

80 – 45 =
= 80 – 50 = 30

943 – 457 =
= 940 – 460 = 480

Page 33

NAME _____

Lesson 2.6 Estimating in the Real World

When adding, round each addend to place value that the numbers have in common.

$$\begin{array}{r} 163 \\ + 48 \end{array} \longrightarrow \begin{array}{r} 160 \\ + 50 \\ \hline 210 \end{array}$$

There are 78 musicians in the band and 32 singers in the chorus at a show. The principal wants to give every member of the band and chorus a flower at the end of the show. Estimate to find about how many flowers the principal needs to buy. Then, solve to find the actual number of flowers the principal needs to buy.

$$\begin{array}{r} 80 \\ + 30 \\ \hline 110 \end{array} \qquad \begin{array}{r} 78 \\ + 32 \\ \hline 110 \end{array}$$

What is the difference between the exact number of flowers and the estimated number of flowers?

$$110 - 110 = 0$$ The difference is 0.

If the principal buys the estimated number, will she have enough flowers to give one to each musician and singer?

Yes. The estimated number and the exact number are the same.

Page 34

NAME _____

Lesson 2.6 Estimating in the Real World

When subtracting, round each number to the greatest place value that the numbers have in common.

$$\begin{array}{r} 163 \\ - 48 \end{array} \longrightarrow \begin{array}{r} 160 \\ - 50 \\ \hline 110 \end{array}$$

Sally is making jewelry for the school craft fair. She has 524 tassels, 2,008 small beads, and 96 large beads.

Sally makes a necklace that has 29 large beads on it. About how many large beads does she have left after making this necklace?

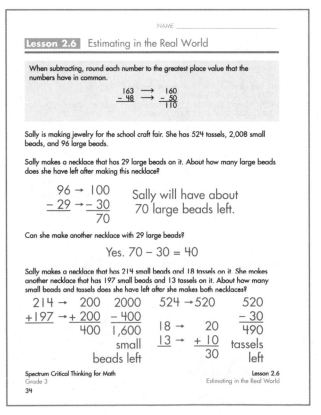

$$\begin{array}{r} 96 \rightarrow 100 \\ - 29 \rightarrow - 30 \\ \hline 70 \end{array}$$ Sally will have about 70 large beads left.

Can she make another necklace with 29 large beads?

Yes. 70 – 30 = 40

Sally makes a necklace that has 214 small beads and 18 tassels on it. She makes another necklace that has 197 small beads and 13 tassels on it. About how many small beads and tassels does she have left after she makes both necklaces?

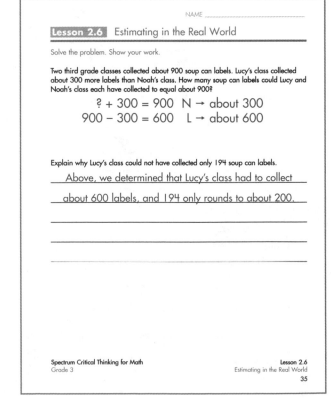

$$\begin{array}{r} 214 \rightarrow 200 \\ +197 \rightarrow + 200 \\ \hline 400 \end{array} \quad \begin{array}{r} 2000 \\ - 400 \\ \hline 1,600 \end{array}$$
small beads left

$$\begin{array}{r} 18 \rightarrow 20 \\ 13 \rightarrow + 10 \\ \hline 30 \end{array}$$

$$\begin{array}{r} 524 \rightarrow 520 \\ - 30 \\ \hline 490 \end{array}$$
tassels left

Page 35

NAME _____

Lesson 2.6 Estimating in the Real World

Solve the problem. Show your work.

Two third grade classes collected about 900 soup can labels. Lucy's class collected about 300 more labels than Noah's class. How many soup can labels could Lucy and Noah's class each have collected to equal about 900?

$$? + 300 = 900 \quad N \rightarrow \text{about } 300$$
$$900 - 300 = 600 \quad L \rightarrow \text{about } 600$$

Explain why Lucy's class could not have collected only 194 soup can labels.

Above, we determined that Lucy's class had to collect
about 600 labels, and 194 only rounds to about 200.

Answer Key

Page 36

NAME _____

Check What You Learned

Adding, Subtracting, and Estimating Through 4-Digit Numbers

1. Jaime earned $195 during her first week of work. She earned $243 during her second week of work. She earned $122 during her third week of work. About how much money did Jaime earn after 3 weeks of work?

$$195 \rightarrow 200$$
$$243 \rightarrow 200$$
$$122 \rightarrow 100$$
$$\overline{\$500}$$

2. At the end of each week, Jamie had to pay $25 for her phone bill and $75 for her groceries. After she paid her bills, exactly how much money did Jaime have each week?

$25	Week 1	Week 2	Week 3
+ 75	$195	$243	$122
$100	− 100	− 100	− 100
	$95	$143	$22

3. After she paid her bills, exactly how much money did Jaime have after 3 weeks?

$$95$$
$$143$$
$$+\ 22$$
$$\overline{\$260}\text{ after 3 weeks}$$

Spectrum Critical Thinking for Math
Grade 3
36

Chapter 2
Check What You Learned

Page 37

NAME _____

Check What You Know

Multiplication and Division

1. Write the rule for the table below. Complete the table.

In	Out
6	12
7	14
8	16
9	18

Multiply by 2

Solve the problems. Show your work.

2. Luis bought 4 boxes of popcorn. Each box has 10 bags of popcorn. How many bags of popcorn does he have? Luis gives 2 bags of popcorn to his neighbor. How many bags of popcorn does Luis have now?

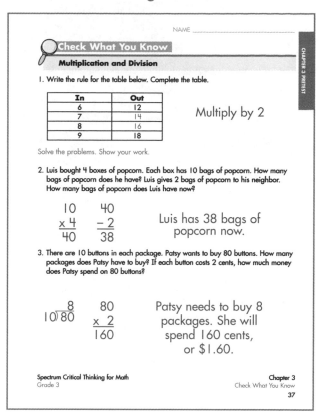

$$\begin{array}{r} 10 \\ \times 4 \\ \hline 40 \end{array} \qquad \begin{array}{r} 40 \\ -\ 2 \\ \hline 38 \end{array}$$

Luis has 38 bags of popcorn now.

3. There are 10 buttons in each package. Patsy wants to buy 80 buttons. How many packages does Patsy have to buy? If each button costs 2 cents, how much money does Patsy spend on 80 buttons?

$$10\overline{)80}\ \ ^{8} \qquad \begin{array}{r} 80 \\ \times\ 2 \\ \hline 160 \end{array}$$

Patsy needs to buy 8 packages. She will spend 160 cents, or $1.60.

Spectrum Critical Thinking for Math
Grade 3
37

Chapter 3
Check What You Know

Page 38

NAME _____

Check What You Know

Multiplication and Division

Find the unknown number in each problem. Write the division or multiplication sentence used to help you.

4. $45 \div \underline{5} = 9$

$$9\overline{)45}\ \ ^{5}$$

5. $72 \div \underline{9} = 8$

$$8\overline{)72}\ \ ^{9}$$

Solve the problems. Show your work.

6. Shane has 24 photos. He wants to arrange them in a rectangle on the wall above his bed. How many rows and columns could he use? Is there another configuration of the same numbers that Shane can use? If so, what is it? Write an equation to show the commutative property.

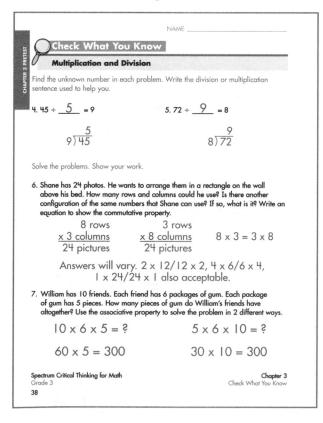

$$\begin{array}{r} 8\text{ rows} \\ \times 3\text{ columns} \\ \hline 24\text{ pictures} \end{array} \qquad \begin{array}{r} 3\text{ rows} \\ \times 8\text{ columns} \\ \hline 24\text{ pictures} \end{array} \qquad 8 \times 3 = 3 \times 8$$

Answers will vary. 2 x 12/12 x 2, 4 x 6/6 x 4, 1 x 24/24 x 1 also acceptable.

7. William has 10 friends. Each friend has 6 packages of gum. Each package of gum has 5 pieces. How many pieces of gum do William's friends have altogether? Use the associative property to solve the problem in 2 different ways.

$$10 \times 6 \times 5 = ? \qquad 5 \times 6 \times 10 = ?$$

$$60 \times 5 = 300 \qquad 30 \times 10 = 300$$

Spectrum Critical Thinking for Math
Grade 3
38

Chapter 3
Check What You Know

Page 39

NAME _____

Lesson 3.1 Understanding Multiplication Topics

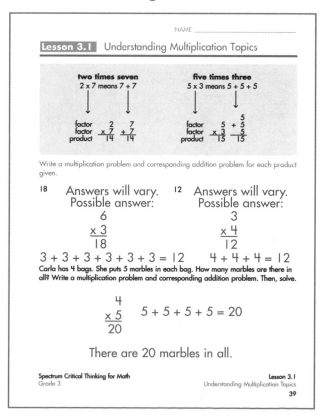

two times seven	**five times three**
2 x 7 means 7 + 7	5 x 3 means 5 + 5 + 5

factor $\begin{array}{r} 2 \\ \text{factor} \times 7 \\ \text{product} \overline{14} \end{array}$ $\begin{array}{r} 7 \\ +\ 7 \\ \hline 14 \end{array}$ factor $\begin{array}{r} 5 \\ \text{factor} \times 3 \\ \text{product} \overline{15} \end{array}$ $\begin{array}{r} 5 \\ +\ 5 \\ 5 \\ \hline 15 \end{array}$

Write a multiplication problem and corresponding addition problem for each product given.

18 Answers will vary. Possible answer:

$$\begin{array}{r} 6 \\ \times 3 \\ \hline 18 \end{array}$$

$$3 + 3 + 3 + 3 + 3 + 3 = 12$$

12 Answers will vary. Possible answer:

$$\begin{array}{r} 3 \\ \times 4 \\ \hline 12 \end{array}$$

$$4 + 4 + 4 = 12$$

Carla has 4 bags. She puts 5 marbles in each bag. How many marbles are there in all? Write a multiplication problem and corresponding addition problem. Then, solve.

$$\begin{array}{r} 4 \\ \times 5 \\ \hline 20 \end{array} \qquad 5 + 5 + 5 + 5 = 20$$

There are 20 marbles in all.

Spectrum Critical Thinking for Math
Grade 3
39

Lesson 3.1
Understanding Multiplication Topics

Answer Key

Page 40

NAME

Lesson 3.2 Understanding Division Topics

$\sqrt{}$ **means divide**   ÷ **also means divide**

divisor ⟶ $3\overline{)18}$ ⟵ quotient
                      ⟵ dividend

$18 \div 3 = 6$

dividend divisor quotient

Write a division problem for each quotient given.

⁴ Answers will vary.   ²⁰ Answers will vary.
   Possible answer: Possible answer:

$2\overline{)8}^{\,4}$ $4\overline{)20}^{\,5}$

David earned $27 for mowing 3 lawns on Saturday. David earned the same amount of money for each lawn. How much did he earn for each lawn? Write a division problem. Then, solve.

$3\overline{)27}^{\,9}$ David earned $9
                          for each lawn.

Spectrum Critical Thinking for Math
Grade 3
40
Lesson 3.2
Understanding Division Topics

Page 41

NAME

Lesson 3.3 Multiplying Through 9 x 9

Multiply the number in each row by the same number in each column. Write the product in the box like the example given. Complete the whole table.

×	1	2	3	4	5	6	7	8	9
1	1	2	3	4	5	6	7	8	9
2	2	4	6	8	10	12	14	16	18
3	3	6	9	12	15	18	21	24	27
4	4	8	12	16	20	24	28	32	36
5	5	10	15	20	25	30	35	40	45
6	6	12	18	24	30	36	42	48	54
7	7	14	21	28	35	42	49	56	63
8	8	16	24	32	40	48	56	64	72
9	9	18	27	36	45	54	63	72	81

Spectrum Critical Thinking for Math
Grade 3
Lesson 3.3
Multiplying Through 9 x 9
41

Page 42

NAME

Lesson 3.3 Multiplying Through 9 x 9

To complete a multiplication table, multiply each number in the **In** column by the same number to get the answer in the **Out** column.

Rule: Multiply by 3

In	Out
3	9
4	12
5	15

Rule: ?

In	Out
3	?
4	16
5	?
6	24

Sometimes, you have to find what the rule is by comparing the **In** and **Out** numbers given.

You can see that 4 x 4 = 16, and 6 x 4 = 24. So, the missing rule for the table above must be **multiply by 4.**

Determine the rule for each table given. Then, complete the table.

In	Out
6	30
7	35
8	40
9	45

Rule: Multiply by 5

In	Out
2	12
3	18
4	24
5	30

Rule: Multiply by 6

Spectrum Critical Thinking for Math
Grade 3
42
Lesson 3.3
Multiplying Through 9 x 9

Page 43

NAME

Lesson 3.4 Multiplying by Multiples of Ten

Use place value to multiply by multiples of ten.

9 x 40 = 9 ones x 4 tens   Multiply 9 ones by 4 tens.

9 x 4 tens = 36 tens = 360   9 x 40 = 360

Solve the problems. Show your work.

Justin read 3 books with 60 pages each. How many pages did he read in all? There were 4 additional pages in the back of each book telling about the next book in the series. If Justin reads those pages, how many total pages will he have read? Write the multiplication problem. Then, solve.

$$\begin{array}{r} 60 \\ \times\ 3 \\ \hline 180 \end{array} \quad \begin{array}{r} 4 \\ \times\ 3 \\ \hline 12 \end{array} \quad \begin{array}{r} 180 \\ +\ 12 \\ \hline 192 \end{array}$$

Justin read 180 pages. If Justin reads the additional 4 pages in the back of each book, he will have read 192 pages.

Wendy used up 4 rolls of stickers. If each roll had 30 stickers, how many stickers did she use in all? Write the multiplication problem. Then, solve.

$$\begin{array}{r} 30 \\ \times\ 4 \\ \hline 120 \end{array}$$

Wendy used 120 stickers in total.

Spectrum Critical Thinking for Math
Grade 3
43
Lesson 3.4
Multiplying by Multiples of Ten

Answer Key

Page 44

NAME _____

Lesson 3.4 Multiplying by Multiples of Ten

Write a word problem to go with each multiplication sentence. Then, solve.

60 x 5 =

$$\begin{array}{r} 60 \\ \times\ 5 \\ \hline 300 \end{array}$$

_____

_____

Word problems will vary.

_____

_____

80 x 5 =

$$\begin{array}{r} 80 \\ \times\ 5 \\ \hline 400 \end{array}$$

_____

Word problems will vary.

_____

_____

_____

Page 45

NAME _____

Lesson 3.5 Division and Multiplication

Multiplication and division are related to each other.

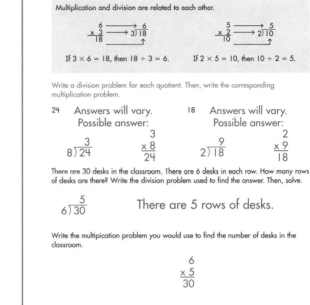

If $3 \times 6 = 18$, then $18 \div 3 = 6$. If $2 \times 5 = 10$, then $10 \div 2 = 5$.

Write a division problem for each quotient. Then, write the corresponding multiplication problem.

24   Answers will vary.
Possible answer:

$$8\overline{)24}\ \ ^{3} \qquad \begin{array}{r}3\\ \times\ 8\\ \hline 24\end{array}$$

18   Answers will vary.
Possible answer:

$$2\overline{)18}\ \ ^{9} \qquad \begin{array}{r}2\\ \times\ 9\\ \hline 18\end{array}$$

There are 30 desks in the classroom. There are 6 desks in each row. How many rows of desks are there? Write the division problem used to find the answer. Then, solve.

$$6\overline{)30}\ \ ^{5} \qquad \text{There are 5 rows of desks.}$$

Write the multipication problem you would use to find the number of desks in the classroom.

$$\begin{array}{r}6\\ \times\ 5\\ \hline 30\end{array}$$

Page 46

NAME _____

Lesson 3.6 Division Problems

Write a word problem for each division problem given. Then, solve.

$$45 \div 9 = \quad 9\overline{)45}\ \ ^{5}$$

_____

Word problems will vary.

_____

_____

$$56 \div 7 = \quad 7\overline{)56}\ \ ^{8}$$

_____

Word problems will vary.

_____

_____

Page 47

NAME _____

Lesson 3.7 Finding Unknowns

To find the missing divisor in a division problem, divide the dividend by the quotient to find your answer.

$14 \div ? = 7 \longrightarrow 14 \div 7 = 2$ Therefore, $14 \div \mathbf{2} = 7$.

To find the missing dividend in a division problem, multiply the divisor by the quotient to find your answer.

$? \div 5 = 4 \longrightarrow 5 \times 4 = 20$ Therefore, $\mathbf{20} \div 5 = 4$.

Find the unknown number in each problem. Write the division or multiplication sentence you used.

$54 \div ? = 6$

$54 \div 6 = 9$
$54 \div 9 = 6$

$? \div 6 = 7$

$7 \times 6 = 42$
$42 \div 7 = 6$

Mrs. Shaw ordered 63 chairs and 7 tables for a banquet. Each table will have the same number of chairs. How many chairs will be at each table? Write the division and multiplication sentences used to solve this problem.

$$7\overline{)63}\ \ ^{9} \qquad 9 \times 7 = 63$$

Each table will have 9 chairs.

At the last minute, Mrs. Shaw had 9 more guests RSVP for the banquet. How many more tables and chairs will she have to order?

She will need 1 more table
and 9 more chairs.

Answer Key

Page 48

Lesson 3.7 Finding Unknowns

To find an unknown factor in a multiplication problem, divide the product by the known factor.

$8 \times ? = 32 \longrightarrow 32 \div 8 = 4$ Therefore, $8 \times 4 = 32$.

$? \times 4 = 32 \longrightarrow 32 \div 4 = 8$ Therefore, $8 \times 4 = 32$.

Find each unknown factor by dividing. Write the division problem. Then, solve.

$7 \times ? = 49$ $? \times 8 = 72$

$7\overline{)49}$ → 7 $8\overline{)72}$ → 9

$7 \times 7 = 49$ $9 \times 8 = 72$

Fiona wants to buy 6 pieces of bubble gum. Each piece costs the same amount. If Fiona spends 30 cents for 6 pieces, how much did each piece cost? Write the multiplication sentence and the division sentence used to solve the problem. Then, solve.

$6\overline{)30}$ → 5 Each piece costs 5 cents.

$5 \times 6 = 30$

Page 49

Lesson 3.7 Finding Unknowns

You can find the unknown factor in a multiplication problem with a multiple of 10 by using place value to divide by multiples of 10.

$? \times 4 = 280 \longrightarrow 28$ tens $\div 4$ ones

28 tens $\div 4$ ones $\longrightarrow 7$ tens $= 70$

$280 \div 4 = 70$

Therefore, $70 \times 4 = 280$.

Find each unknown factor by dividing. Write the division problem. Then, solve.

$? \times 6 = 480$ $30 \times ? = 270$

$6\overline{)48 \text{ tens}}$ → 8 ones $3 \text{ tens}\overline{)27 \text{ tens}}$ → 9 ones

$80 \times 6 = 480$ $30 \times 9 = 270$

There are 10 apples in each basket. Paige wants to buy 60 apples. How many baskets of apples does Paige have to buy? Write the division problem used to solve. Then, solve.

$10\overline{)60}$ → 6 Paige has to buy 6 baskets of apples.

If each apple costs 3 cents, how much money does Paige spend on 60 apples?

$3 \times 60 = 180$

Paige will spend 180 cents, or $1.80, on 60 apples.

Page 50

Lesson 3.8 Multistep Word Problems

The PE teacher gave each team 6 basketballs and 6 tennis balls. If there were 5 teams, how many total balls did the PE teacher give out?

Each team gets 6 of each type of ball. I know that 5 times 6 is 30, so that is 30 basketballs and 30 tennis balls. Then, I can add the balls together, and 30 plus 30 is 60. So, there are 60 balls in all.

$\begin{array}{r}5\\\times 6\\\hline 30\end{array}$ $\begin{array}{r}30\\+30\\\hline 60\end{array}$

Solve the problems. Show your work

9 girls and 6 boys each have an eraser collection. Each girl has 7 erasers in her collection, and each boy has 5 erasers in his collection. How many erasers altogether do the boys and girls have?

$\begin{array}{r}9\\\times 7\\\hline 63\end{array}$ $\begin{array}{r}6\\\times 5\\\hline 30\end{array}$ $\begin{array}{r}63\\+30\\\hline 93\end{array}$

Altogether, the boys and girls have 93 erasers.

Brooke bought 8 boxes of chocolate chip cookies and 6 boxes of peanut butter cookies. Each box of chocolate chip cookies has 9 cookies. Each box of peanut butter cookies has 8 cookies. How many cookies does Brooke have altogether?

$\begin{array}{r}8\\\times 9\\\hline 72\end{array}$ $\begin{array}{r}6\\\times 8\\\hline 48\end{array}$ $\begin{array}{r}72\\+48\\\hline 120\end{array}$

Altogether, Brooke has 120 cookies.

Page 51

Lesson 3.8 Multistep Word Problems

Quincey earned 6 stickers a day for 9 days. After 9 days, he gave away 5 stickers to his best friend Tony. Then, he divided the rest of his stickers up between his 7 brothers. If each brother got the same number of stickers, how many stickers did each brother get?

$\begin{array}{r}6\\\times 9\\\hline 54\end{array}$ $\begin{array}{r}54\\-5\\\hline 49\end{array}$ $7\overline{)49}$ → 7

Quincey gave each brother 7 stickers.

James, Joseph, and Judd combined all of their toy cars. James had 21 cars, Joseph had 35, and Judd had 16. They wanted to donate an equal number of toys to 9 friends. How many toy cars did each friend get?

$\begin{array}{r}21\\35\\+16\\\hline 72\end{array}$ $9\overline{)72}$ → 8

Each friend got 8 toy cars.

Hunter read 35 pages of his book on Friday and 52 pages of his book on Saturday. The book is 105 pages long. If he wants to finish the remaining pages in 2 days, how many pages must he read each day?

$\begin{array}{r}35\\+52\\\hline 87\end{array}$ $\begin{array}{r}105\\-87\\\hline 18\end{array}$ $2\overline{)18}$ → 9

Hunter needs to read 9 pages each day.

Answer Key

Page 52

NAME _____

Lesson 3.9 Identity and Commutative Properties

Identity Property	**Commutative Property**
for addition: $3 + 0 = 3$	for addition: $3 + 2 = 2 + 3$
for multiplication: $3 \times 1 = 3$	for multiplication: $4 \times 3 = 3 \times 4$

A number sentence can change its look but not change its value.

$3 + 5 = 8$ **or** $3 + 5 = 4 + 4$ $3 \times 8 = 24$ **or** $3 \times 8 = 6 \times 4$

For each answer, write 2 different number sentences showing the identity property. Include at least 1 multiplication number sentence.

8
$$8 + 0 = 8$$
$$8 \times 1 = 8$$

15
$$15 + 0 = 15$$
$$15 \times 1 = 15$$

For each answer, write a number sentence showing the commutative property for addition.

For each answer, write a number sentence showing the commutative property for multiplication.

18   Answers will vary. Possible answer:
$$10 + 8 = 8 + 10$$

12   Answers will vary. Possible answer:
$$4 \times 3 = 3 \times 4$$

12   Answers will vary. Possible answer:
$$4 + 8 = 8 + 4$$

18   Answers will vary. Possible answer:
$$9 \times 2 = 2 \times 9$$

Page 53

NAME _____

Lesson 3.10 Associative and Distributive Properties

Associative Property	**Distributive Property**
Addition:	
$(1 + 2) + 3 = 1 + (2 + 3)$	$2 \times 7 = 2 \times (3 + 4) = (2 \times 3) + (2 \times 4)$
Multiplication:	
$(1 \times 2) \times 3 = 1 \times (2 \times 3)$	

Solve the problems. Show your work.

Kevin and Leslie play a missing-number game. They write number sentences that have parentheses on both sides of the equal sign. They leave one number missing from each sentence.

Help Kevin find the missing number in Leslie's number sentence.

$(15 + 6) + 12 = (12 + 6) + \underline{15}$

Help Leslie find the missing number in Kevin's number sentence.

$(2 \times 2) \times \underline{6} = (2 \times 6) \times 2$

Write a number sentence that totals **81** to demonstrate the associative property.

Answers will vary. Possible answer:
$$(20 + 30) + 31 = 20 + (30 + 31)$$

Write 2 number sentences (addition and multiplication) that each total **64** to demonstrate the distributive property.

Answers will vary. Possible answers:
$$8 \times 8 = (2 \times 8) + (6 \times 8)$$
$$4 \times 16 = (2 \times 16) + (2 \times 16)$$

Page 54

NAME _____

💡 **Check What You Learned**

Multiplication and Division

1. There are 7 girls on stage. Each girl is holding 9 flowers. How many flowers are there in all? If 21 flowers are white, 21 flowers are red, and the rest are pink, how many flowers are pink?

$$9 \times 7 = 63$$
There are 63 flowers in total.
$$21 + 21 = 42$$
$$63 - 42 = 21$$
21 of the flowers are pink.

2. During a tournament, 2 teams play against each other. There are 10 players on the field for each team. How many players are on the field during the game? There are 8 fields at the park where the tournament is held. How many total players are on all 8 fields?

$$10 \times 2 = 20$$
20 players are on the field during the game.
$$20 \times 8 = 160$$
160 players are on all 8 fields in total.

3. Write the rule for the table. Complete the table.

In	Out
4	28
5	35
6	42
7	49
8	56

Multiply by 7

CHAPTER 3 POSTTEST

Page 55

NAME _____

💡 **Check What You Learned**

Multiplication and Division

4. 18 fish were caught on a deep-sea fishing boat. If each person on the boat caught 2 fish, how many people were on the boat?

$$18 \div 2 = 9$$
9 people

5. Write the multiplication problem you would use to calculate how many fish were caught.

2 fish x 9 people = 18 fish

6. Shanette has 41 erasers, and Zoe gives her 7 more. Shanette gives each of her 8 friends an equal number of erasers. How many erasers does each friend get?

$$41 + 7 = 48$$
$$48 \div 8 = 6$$
6 erasers

7. One of Shanette's friends does not want erasers and decides to divide hers among the 7 friends. Will she be able to do this? Explain your answer.

No, she only has 6 erasers and therefore cannot give at least 1 eraser to each of her 7 friends.

CHAPTER 3 POSTTEST

Answer Key

Page 56

NAME _____

Mid-Test Chapters 1–3

Solve the problems. Show your work.

1. Pablo's favorite book is *Traveling Without Shoes*. The book has 845 pages of text and 79 pages of pictures. If Pablo is on page 514, how many more pages until he gets to the end of the book?

$$845 + 79 = 942$$
$$924 - 514 = 410$$
410 pages

2. Vanessa is reading a book that has 692 pages. She reads 271 pages on Saturday and 287 pages on Sunday. About how many pages does Vanessa read on Saturday and Sunday?

$$300 + 300 = 600$$
About 600 pages

3. Vanessa wants to finish the book on Monday. About how many pages will she need to read?

$$700 - 600 = 100$$
About 100 pages

4. Ramsey took pictures of 64 animals at the zoo. He took 15 pictures of giraffes, 24 pictures of lions, and 12 pictures of pandas. How many pictures of other animals did he take?

$$15 + 24 + 12 = 51$$
$$64 - 51 = 13$$
He took 13 pictures of other animals.

Spectrum Critical Thinking for Math
Grade 3
56

Chapters 1–3
Mid-Test

Page 57

NAME _____

Mid-Test Chapters 1–3

Solve the problems. Show your work.

5. Tyler went on a hiking trip. He started his trip at an elevation of 1,111 feet. After 3 days of hiking, he reached 6,389 feet. About how many feet did Tyler climb over 3 days?

$$6,000 - 1,000 = 5,000$$
5,000 feet

6. If Tyler stopped to rest on the second day at an elevation of 4,220 feet, exactly how far did he climb the first 2 days?

$$4,220 - 1,111 = 3,109$$
3,109 feet

7. How far did Tyler climb the third day?

$$6,389 - 1,111 = 5,278$$
$$5,278 - 3,109 = 2,169$$
He climbed 2,169 feet the third day.

8. Lola needs 415 balloons for a party. She has 179 balloons and her mom gives her 134 more. Does Lola have enough balloons for the party? If not, how many more does she need?

$$179 + 134 = 313$$
$$415 - 313 = 102$$
No, she needs 102 more balloons.

Spectrum Critical Thinking for Math
Grade 3

Chapters 1–3
Mid-Test
57

Page 58

NAME _____

Mid-Test Chapters 1–3

9. Write the rule. Complete the table.

In	Out
6	48
7	56
8	64
9	72

Multiply by 8

10. Blake has 100 apples. She has 20 friends. She gave each friend 3 apples. How many apples did Blake give away?

$$20 \times 3 = 60$$ Blake gave away 60 apples.

11. It takes 10 apples to make a pie. How many pies can Blake make with the apples that she has left?

$$100 - 60 = 40; 40 \div 10 = 4$$ Blake can make 4 pies.

Eight friends want a new gaming system. The system costs $89. Each friend has $5.

12. Will they have enough money to buy the gaming system?

$$5 \times 8 = 40$$ No, they will not have enough.

13. If they don't have enough, how much more do they need?

$$89 - 40 = 49$$ They need $49 more.

14. How many more friends with $5 would they need?

$$5 \times 10 = 50$$
$$50 > 49$$ They would need 10 more friends.

Spectrum Critical Thinking for Math
Grade 3
58

Chapters 1–3
Mid-Test

Page 59

NAME _____

Mid-Test Chapters 1–3

Solve the problems. Show your work.

15. There are 24 skiers waiting in line for the ski lift. 3 skiers can sit in each seat on the lift. How many seats are needed for all of the skiers?

$$3\overline{)24}^{\,8}$$ 8 seats are needed.

16. If 1 skier decides to get out of line, how does this affect the number of seats needed for the skiers?

If 1 skier leaves, they will still need 8 seats, but the eighth seat will only hold 2 skiers.

Abigail helps get 6 sailboats ready for a sailing class. She divides the supplies evenly between each sailboat. She has 12 sails and 30 life jackets. All of the sailboats need new ropes for their sails. Each boat needs 4 pieces of rope.

17. How many sails go on each boat?

$$12 \div 6 = 2$$ 2 sails go on each boat.

18. How many life jackets go on each boat?

$$30 \div 6 = 5$$ 5 life jackets go on each boat.

19. How many pieces of rope does Abigail need?

$$4 \times 6 = 24$$ Abigail needs 24 pieces of rope.

Spectrum Critical Thinking for Math
Grade 3

Chapters 1–3
Mid-Test
59

Answer Key

Page 60

NAME _____

Check What You Know

Fractions

Divide each shape into the equal parts shown. Then, shade the fraction given.

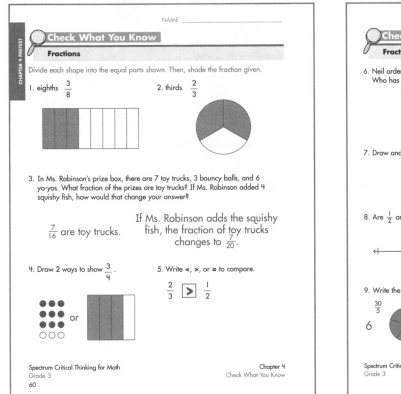

1. eighths $\frac{3}{8}$

2. thirds $\frac{2}{3}$

3. In Ms. Robinson's prize box, there are 7 toy trucks, 3 bouncy balls, and 6 yo-yos. What fraction of the prizes are toy trucks? If Ms. Robinson added 4 squishy fish, how would that change your answer?

$\frac{7}{16}$ are toy trucks.

If Ms. Robinson adds the squishy fish, the fraction of toy trucks changes to $\frac{7}{20}$.

4. Draw 2 ways to show $\frac{3}{4}$.

5. Write <, >, or = to compare.

$\frac{2}{3}$ **>** $\frac{1}{2}$

Spectrum Critical Thinking for Math
Grade 3
60

Chapter 4
Check What You Know

Page 61

NAME _____

Check What You Know

Fractions

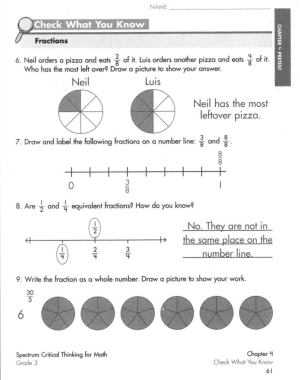

6. Neil orders a pizza and eats $\frac{2}{8}$ of it. Luis orders another pizza and eats $\frac{4}{8}$ of it. Who has the most left over? Draw a picture to show your answer.

Neil   Luis

Neil has the most leftover pizza.

7. Draw and label the following fractions on a number line: $\frac{3}{8}$ and $\frac{8}{8}$.

8. Are $\frac{1}{2}$ and $\frac{1}{4}$ equivalent fractions? How do you know?

No. They are not in the same place on the number line.

9. Write the fraction as a whole number. Draw a picture to show your work.

$\frac{30}{5}$

6

Spectrum Critical Thinking for Math
Grade 3
61

Chapter 4
Check What You Know

Page 62

Lesson 4.1 Parts of a Whole

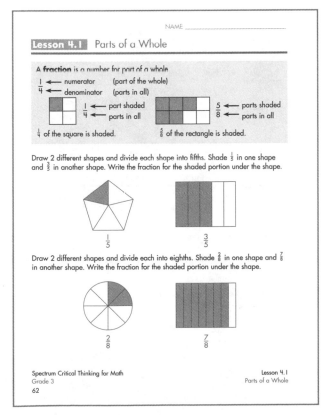

A **fraction** is a number for part of a whole.

$\frac{1}{4}$ ← numerator (part of the whole)
  ← denominator (parts in all)

$\frac{1}{4}$ ← part shaded
  ← parts in all

$\frac{1}{4}$ of the square is shaded.

$\frac{5}{8}$ ← parts shaded
  ← parts in all

$\frac{5}{8}$ of the rectangle is shaded.

Draw 2 different shapes and divide each shape into fifths. Shade $\frac{1}{5}$ in one shape and $\frac{3}{5}$ in another shape. Write the fraction for the shaded portion under the shape.

$\frac{1}{5}$ $\frac{3}{5}$

Draw 2 different shapes and divide each into eighths. Shade $\frac{2}{8}$ in one shape and $\frac{7}{8}$ in another shape. Write the fraction for the shaded portion under the shape.

$\frac{2}{8}$ $\frac{7}{8}$

Spectrum Critical Thinking for Math
Grade 3
62

Lesson 4.1
Parts of a Whole

Page 63

Lesson 4.2 Parts of a Set

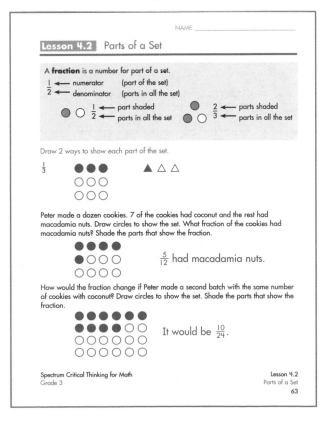

A **fraction** is a number for part of a set.

$\frac{1}{2}$ ← numerator (part of the set)
  ← denominator (parts in all the set)

$\frac{1}{2}$ ← part shaded
  ← parts in all the set

$\frac{2}{3}$ ← parts shaded
  ← parts in all the set

Draw 2 ways to show each part of the set.

$\frac{1}{3}$

Peter made a dozen cookies. 7 of the cookies had coconut and the rest had macadamia nuts. Draw circles to show the set. What fraction of the cookies had macadamia nuts? Shade the parts that show the fraction.

$\frac{5}{12}$ had macadamia nuts.

How would the fraction change if Peter made a second batch with the same number of cookies with coconut? Draw circles to show the set. Shade the parts that show the fraction.

It would be $\frac{10}{24}$.

Spectrum Critical Thinking for Math
Grade 3
63

Lesson 4.2
Parts of a Set

Answer Key

Page 64

Lesson 4.3 Comparing Fractions

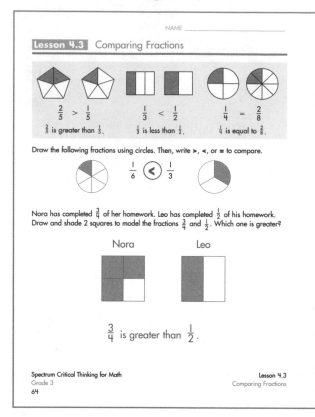

$\frac{2}{5} > \frac{1}{5}$

$\frac{2}{5}$ is greater than $\frac{1}{5}$.

$\frac{1}{3} < \frac{1}{2}$

$\frac{1}{3}$ is less than $\frac{1}{2}$.

$\frac{1}{4} = \frac{2}{8}$

$\frac{1}{4}$ is equal to $\frac{2}{8}$.

Draw the following fractions using circles. Then, write >, <, or = to compare.

$\frac{1}{6} < \frac{1}{3}$

Nora has completed $\frac{3}{4}$ of her homework. Leo has completed $\frac{1}{2}$ of his homework. Draw and shade 2 squares to model the fractions $\frac{3}{4}$ and $\frac{1}{2}$. Which one is greater?

Nora   Leo

$\frac{3}{4}$ is greater than $\frac{1}{2}$.

Page 65

Lesson 4.3 Comparing Fractions

Write <, >, or = to compare.

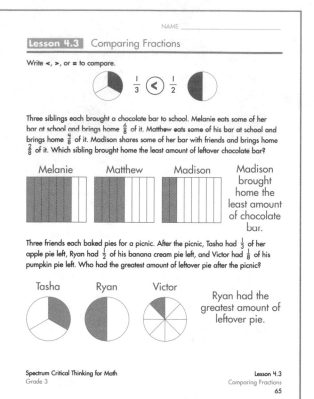

$\frac{1}{3} < \frac{1}{2}$

Three siblings each brought a chocolate bar to school. Melanie eats some of her bar at school and brings home $\frac{6}{8}$ of it. Matthew eats some of his bar at school and brings home $\frac{4}{8}$ of it. Madison shares some of her bar with friends and brings home $\frac{2}{8}$ of it. Which sibling brought home the least amount of leftover chocolate bar?

Melanie   Matthew   Madison

Madison brought home the least amount of chocolate bar.

Three friends each baked pies for a picnic. After the picnic, Tasha had $\frac{1}{3}$ of her apple pie left, Ryan had $\frac{1}{2}$ of his banana cream pie left, and Victor had $\frac{1}{8}$ of his pumpkin pie left. Who had the greatest amount of leftover pie after the picnic?

Tasha   Ryan   Victor

Ryan had the greatest amount of leftover pie.

Page 66

Lesson 4.4 Fractions on a Number Line

Label $\frac{1}{8}$ on a number line.

First, divide the number line into 8 equal parts (the denominator).
Next, count from zero the parts you need (the numerator).
Finally, label the fraction.

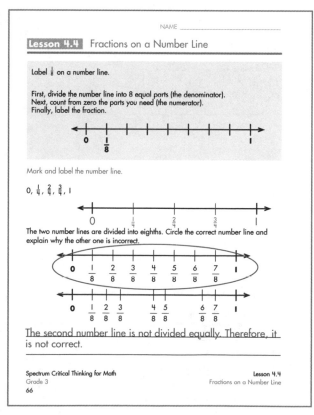

Mark and label the number line.

$0, \frac{1}{4}, \frac{2}{4}, \frac{3}{4}, 1$

The two number lines are divided into eighths. Circle the correct number line and explain why the other one is incorrect.

The second number line is not divided equally. Therefore, it is not correct.

Page 67

Lesson 4.4 Fractions on a Number Line

The fractions $\frac{2}{4}$ and $\frac{1}{2}$ are equivalent because they are at the same spot on the number line.

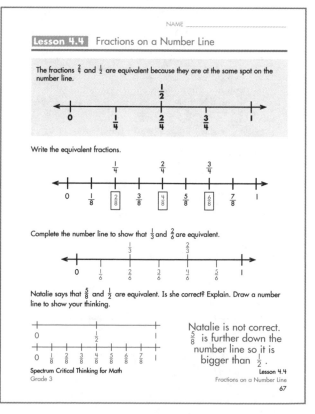

Write the equivalent fractions.

Complete the number line to show that $\frac{1}{3}$ and $\frac{2}{6}$ are equivalent.

Natalie says that $\frac{5}{8}$ and $\frac{1}{2}$ are equivalent. Is she correct? Explain. Draw a number line to show your thinking.

Natalie is not correct. $\frac{5}{8}$ is further down the number line so it is bigger than $\frac{1}{2}$.

Answer Key

Page 68

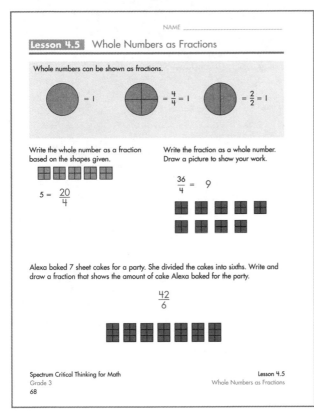

NAME _____

Lesson 4.5 Whole Numbers as Fractions

Whole numbers can be shown as fractions.

Write the whole number as a fraction based on the shapes given.

$5 = \dfrac{20}{4}$

Write the fraction as a whole number. Draw a picture to show your work.

$\dfrac{36}{4} = 9$

Alexa baked 7 sheet cakes for a party. She divided the cakes into sixths. Write and draw a fraction that shows the amount of cake Alexa baked for the party.

$\dfrac{42}{6}$

Page 69

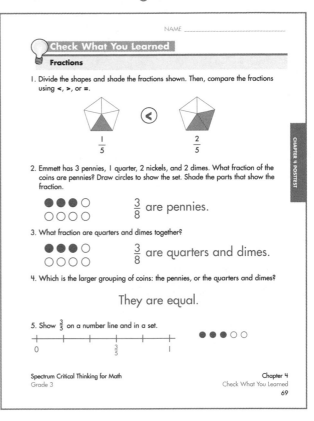

NAME _____

Check What You Learned

Fractions

1. Divide the shapes and shade the fractions shown. Then, compare the fractions using <, >, or =.

$\dfrac{1}{5}$ (<) $\dfrac{2}{5}$

2. Emmett has 3 pennies, 1 quarter, 2 nickels, and 2 dimes. What fraction of the coins are pennies? Draw circles to show the set. Shade the parts that show the fraction.

$\dfrac{3}{8}$ are pennies.

3. What fraction are quarters and dimes together?

$\dfrac{3}{8}$ are quarters and dimes.

4. Which is the larger grouping of coins: the pennies, or the quarters and dimes?

They are equal.

5. Show $\dfrac{3}{5}$ on a number line and in a set.

CHAPTER 4 POSTTEST

Page 70

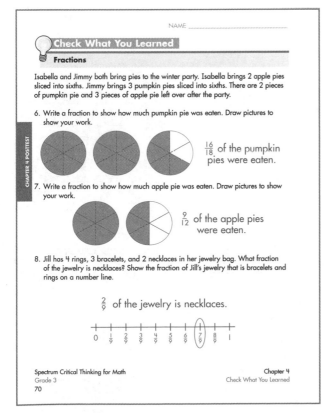

NAME _____

Check What You Learned

Fractions

Isabella and Jimmy both bring pies to the winter party. Isabella brings 2 apple pies sliced into sixths. Jimmy brings 3 pumpkin pies sliced into sixths. There are 2 pieces of pumpkin pie and 3 pieces of apple pie left over after the party.

6. Write a fraction to show how much pumpkin pie was eaten. Draw pictures to show your work.

$\dfrac{16}{18}$ of the pumpkin pies were eaten.

7. Write a fraction to show how much apple pie was eaten. Draw pictures to show your work.

$\dfrac{9}{12}$ of the apple pies were eaten.

8. Jill has 4 rings, 3 bracelets, and 2 necklaces in her jewelry bag. What fraction of the jewelry is necklaces? Show the fraction of Jill's jewelry that is bracelets and rings on a number line.

$\dfrac{2}{9}$ of the jewelry is necklaces.

CHAPTER 4 POSTTEST

Page 71

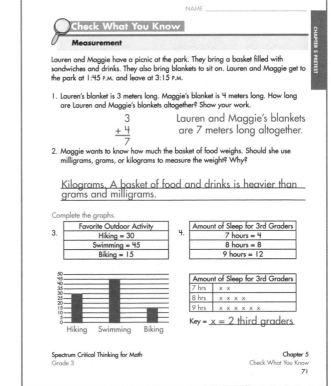

NAME _____

Check What You Know

Measurement

Lauren and Maggie have a picnic at the park. They bring a basket filled with sandwiches and drinks. They also bring blankets to sit on. Lauren and Maggie get to the park at 1:45 P.M. and leave at 3:15 P.M.

1. Lauren's blanket is 3 meters long. Maggie's blanket is 4 meters long. How long are Lauren and Maggie's blankets altogether? Show your work.

$\begin{array}{r} 3 \\ + 4 \\ \hline 7 \end{array}$

Lauren and Maggie's blankets are 7 meters long altogether.

2. Maggie wants to know how much the basket of food weighs. Should she use milligrams, grams, or kilograms to measure the weight? Why?

Kilograms. A basket of food and drinks is heavier than grams and milligrams.

Complete the graphs.

3.

Favorite Outdoor Activity
Hiking = 30
Swimming = 45
Biking = 15

4.

Amount of Sleep for 3rd Graders
7 hours = 4
8 hours = 8
9 hours = 12

Amount of Sleep for 3rd Graders	
7 hrs	x x
8 hrs	x x x x
9 hrs	x x x x x x

Key = x = 2 third graders

CHAPTER 5 PRETEST

Answer Key

Page 72

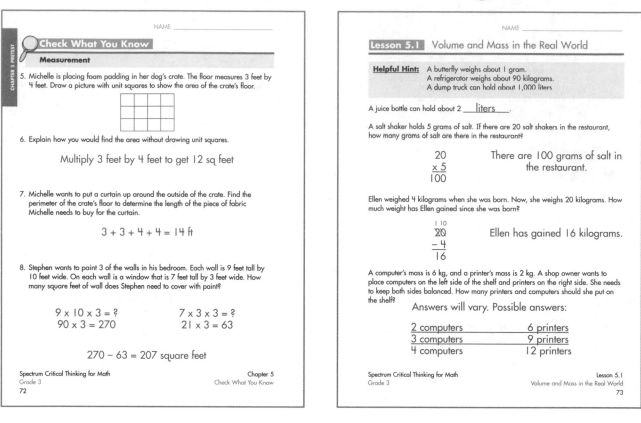

CHAPTER 5 PRETEST

NAME _____

Check What You Know

Measurement

5. Michelle is placing foam padding in her dog's crate. The floor measures 3 feet by 4 feet. Draw a picture with unit squares to show the area of the crate's floor.

6. Explain how you would find the area without drawing unit squares.

Multiply 3 feet by 4 feet to get 12 sq feet

7. Michelle wants to put a curtain up around the outside of the crate. Find the perimeter of the crate's floor to determine the length of the piece of fabric Michelle needs to buy for the curtain.

3 + 3 + 4 + 4 = 14 ft

8. Stephen wants to paint 3 of the walls in his bedroom. Each wall is 9 feet tall by 10 feet wide. On each wall is a window that is 7 feet tall by 3 feet wide. How many square feet of wall does Stephen need to cover with paint?

9 x 10 x 3 = ?   7 x 3 x 3 = ?
90 x 3 = 270   21 x 3 = 63

270 – 63 = 207 square feet

Spectrum Critical Thinking for Math
Grade 3
72

Chapter 5
Check What You Know

Page 73

NAME _____

Lesson 5.1 Volume and Mass in the Real World

Helpful Hint: A butterfly weighs about 1 gram.
A refrigerator weighs about 90 kilograms.
A dump truck can hold about 1,000 liters.

A juice bottle can hold about 2 ____liters____ .

A salt shaker holds 5 grams of salt. If there are 20 salt shakers in the restaurant, how many grams of salt are there in the restaurant?

$$\begin{array}{r} 20 \\ \times 5 \\ \hline 100 \end{array}$$

There are 100 grams of salt in the restaurant.

Ellen weighed 4 kilograms when she was born. Now, she weighs 20 kilograms. How much weight has Ellen gained since she was born?

$$\begin{array}{r} {}^{1\ 10} \\ \cancel{20} \\ -\ 4 \\ \hline 16 \end{array}$$

Ellen has gained 16 kilograms.

A computer's mass is 6 kg, and a printer's mass is 2 kg. A shop owner wants to place computers on the left side of the shelf and printers on the right side. She needs to keep both sides balanced. How many printers and computers should she put on the shelf?

Answers will vary. Possible answers:

2 computers   6 printers
3 computers   9 printers
4 computers   12 printers

Spectrum Critical Thinking for Math
Grade 3

Lesson 5.1
Volume and Mass in the Real World
73

Page 74

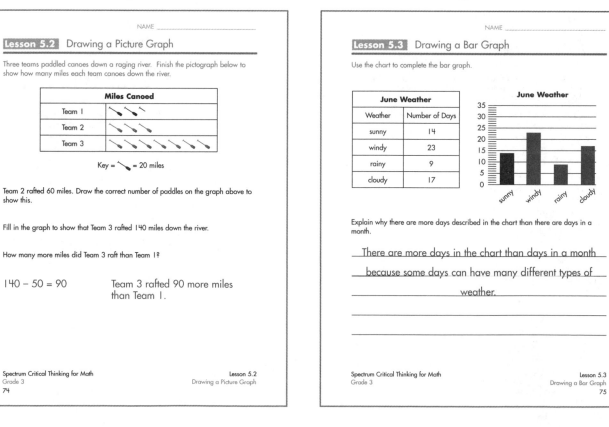

NAME _____

Lesson 5.2 Drawing a Picture Graph

Three teams paddled canoes down a raging river. Finish the pictograph below to show how many miles each team canoes down the river.

Miles Canoed

Team 1	
Team 2	
Team 3	

Key = ✎ = 20 miles

Team 2 rafted 60 miles. Draw the correct number of paddles on the graph above to show this.

Fill in the graph to show that Team 3 rafted 140 miles down the river.

How many more miles did Team 3 raft than Team 1?

140 – 50 = 90   Team 3 rafted 90 more miles than Team 1.

Spectrum Critical Thinking for Math
Grade 3
74

Lesson 5.2
Drawing a Picture Graph

Page 75

NAME _____

Lesson 5.3 Drawing a Bar Graph

Use the chart to complete the bar graph.

June Weather

Weather	Number of Days
sunny	14
windy	23
rainy	9
cloudy	17

June Weather

Explain why there are more days described in the chart than there are days in a month.

There are more days in the chart than days in a month because some days can have many different types of weather.

Spectrum Critical Thinking for Math
Grade 3

Lesson 5.3
Drawing a Bar Graph
75

Answer Key

Page 76

NAME _____

Lesson 5.4 Gather Data to Draw a Line Plot

Use a ruler to measure the length of each object to the nearest quarter inch.

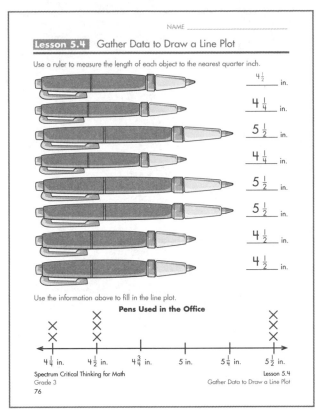

$4\frac{1}{2}$ in.

$4\frac{1}{4}$ in.

$5\frac{1}{2}$ in.

$4\frac{1}{4}$ in.

$5\frac{1}{2}$ in.

$5\frac{1}{2}$ in.

$4\frac{1}{2}$ in.

$4\frac{1}{2}$ in.

Use the information above to fill in the line plot.

Pens Used in the Office

```
  X           X                                    X
  X           X                                    X X
  |-----------|-----------|-----------|-----------|-----------|
4¼ in.      4½ in.      4¾ in.       5 in.      5¼ in.      5½ in.
```

Page 77

NAME _____

Lesson 5.5 Finding Area with Unit Squares

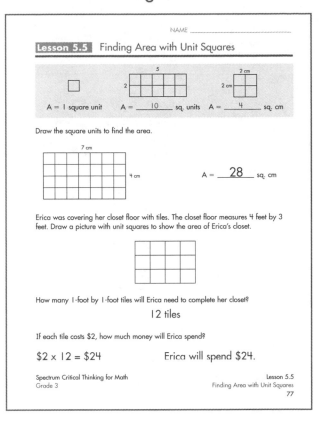

A = 1 square unit   A = __10__ sq. units   A = __4__ sq. cm

Draw the square units to find the area.

7 cm

4 cm

A = __28__ sq. cm

Erica was covering her closet floor with tiles. The closet floor measures 4 feet by 3 feet. Draw a picture with unit squares to show the area of Erica's closet.

How many 1-foot by 1-foot tiles will Erica need to complete her closet?

12 tiles

If each tile costs $2, how much money will Erica spend?

$2 x 12 = $24   Erica will spend $24.

Page 78

NAME _____

Lesson 5.6 Area of Regular Shapes

To find the area of a square or rectangle, multiply length by width.

10 ft. × 2 ft. = 20 sq. ft.

10 ft. (length)
2 ft. (width)

The product is written as 20 square feet.

Orlando puts down 40 square feet of carpet in his rectangle-shaped bedroom. What could the dimensions of his bedroom be? Draw a picture and label it to show your thinking.

Answers will vary. Possible answer:

10 ft.
4 ft.

Denise wants to plant tulips, daffodils, and hydrangeas in a rectangular garden that is 30 feet long by 7 feet wide. The tulips should take up at least 30 square feet. The daffodils should take up no more than 35 square feet. The hydrangeas should take up 70 square feet. Denise also wants to leave a 1-foot-wide border around the edge of the garden. Draw a diagram to show one way Denise could design her garden.

Answers will vary. Possible answer:

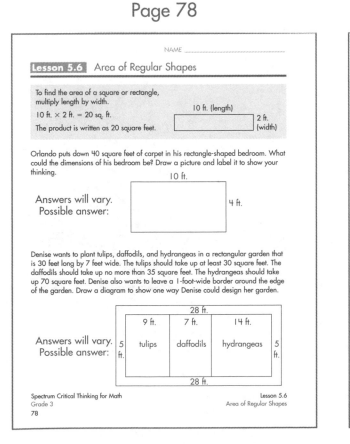

28 ft.

9 ft.	7 ft.	14 ft.
tulips	daffodils	hydrangeas

5 ft.   5 ft.

28 ft.

Page 79

NAME _____

Lesson 5.6 Area of Regular Shapes

Draw the square units.   Multiply to check your answer.

3 cm
5 cm

__5__ × __3__ = __15__

A = __15__ sq. cm

A = __15__ sq. cm

Draw the square units. Then, multiply to check your answer.

9 in.
3 in

__9__ × __3__ = __27__

A = __27__ sq. in.

Sean wants to tile the kitchen floor. The kitchen floor measures 6 feet wide by 10 feet long. The tile store has high-grade tile, which costs $8 per square foot; mid-grade tile, which costs $5 per square foot; and low-grade tile, which costs $3 per square foot.

How many 1-foot square tiles will Sean need to tile his kitchen?

6 x 10 = 60   He will need 60 tiles.

How much will Sean pay for each type of tile?

High: $8 x 60 = $480
Mid: $5 x 60 = $300
Low: $3 x 60 = $180

Answer Key

Page 80

Lesson 5.7 Area of Irregular Shapes

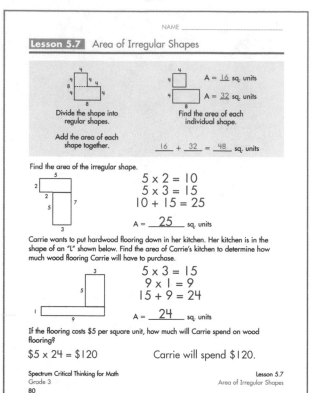

Divide the shape into regular shapes.

A = _16_ sq. units

Find the area of each individual shape.

A = _32_ sq. units

Add the area of each shape together.

_16_ + _32_ = _48_ sq. units

Find the area of the irregular shape.

$5 \times 2 = 10$
$5 \times 3 = 15$
$10 + 15 = 25$

A = ___25___ sq. units

Carrie wants to put hardwood flooring down in her kitchen. Her kitchen is in the shape of an "L" shown below. Find the area of Carrie's kitchen to determine how much wood flooring Carrie will have to purchase.

$5 \times 3 = 15$
$9 \times 1 = 9$
$15 + 9 = 24$

A = ___24___ sq. units

If the flooring costs $5 per square unit, how much will Carrie spend on wood flooring?

$5 × 24 = $120   Carrie will spend $120.

Page 81

Lesson 5.7 Area of Irregular Shapes

Find the area of each irregular shape.

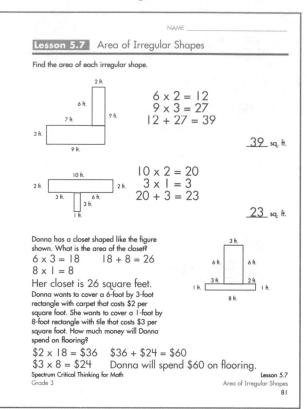

$6 \times 2 = 12$
$9 \times 3 = 27$
$12 + 27 = 39$

___39___ sq. ft.

$10 \times 2 = 20$
$3 \times 1 = 3$
$20 + 3 = 23$

___23___ sq. ft.

Donna has a closet shaped like the figure shown. What is the area of the closet?

$6 \times 3 = 18$ $18 + 8 = 26$
$8 \times 1 = 8$

Her closet is 26 square feet.

Donna wants to cover a 6-foot by 3-foot rectangle with carpet that costs $2 per square foot. She wants to cover a 1-foot by 8-foot rectangle with tile that costs $3 per square foot. How much money will Donna spend on flooring?

$2 × 18 = $36 $36 + $24 = $60
$3 × 8 = $24   Donna will spend $60 on flooring.

Page 82

Lesson 5.8 Measuring Perimeter

Perimeter is the distance around a shape.

To calculate perimeter, add together the lengths of all the sides.

Perimeter = 17 in. + 10 in. + 17 in. + 10 in.

Perimeter = 54 in.

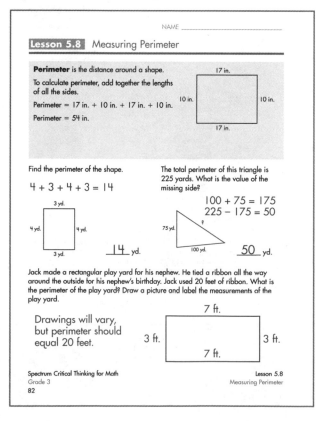

Find the perimeter of the shape.

$4 + 3 + 4 + 3 = 14$

___14___ yd.

The total perimeter of this triangle is 225 yards. What is the value of the missing side?

$100 + 75 = 175$
$225 - 175 = 50$

___50___ yd.

Jack made a rectangular play yard for his nephew. He tied a ribbon all the way around the outside for his nephew's birthday. Jack used 20 feet of ribbon. What is the perimeter of the play yard? Draw a picture and label the measurements of the play yard.

Drawings will vary, but perimeter should equal 20 feet.

7 ft.
3 ft.   3 ft.
7 ft.

Page 83

Lesson 5.9 Time

5:15 is read "five fifteen" and means "15 minutes after 5."

12:50 is read "twelve fifty" and means "50 minutes after 12" or "10 minutes to 1."

4:45 is read "four forty-five" and means "45 minutes after 4" or "15 minutes to 5."

Draw the hands on the analog clock and write the time in the digital clock to show the time described.

one ten

1:10

seven fifty-five

7:55

Laura leaves for work at 8:05 A.M. She drives for 40 minutes. What time does she get to work?

Laura gets to work at 8:45 A.M.

Laura has one hour for lunch. She leaves work at 12:00 P.M. and drives for 15 minutes to a restaurant. She spends 30 minutes eating lunch. Then, she drives for 15 minutes back to work. What time does she get back to work?

Laura gets back to work at 1:00 P.M.

Answer Key

Page 84

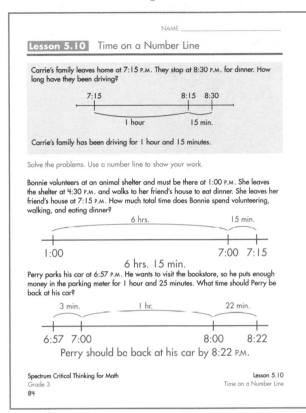

Lesson 5.10 Time on a Number Line

Carrie's family leaves home at 7:15 P.M. They stop at 8:30 P.M. for dinner. How long have they been driving?

7:15   8:15   8:30

1 hour   15 min.

Carrie's family has been driving for 1 hour and 15 minutes.

Solve the problems. Use a number line to show your work.

Bonnie volunteers at an animal shelter and must be there at 1:00 P.M. She leaves the shelter at 4:30 P.M. and walks to her friend's house to eat dinner. She leaves her friend's house at 7:15 P.M. How much total time does Bonnie spend volunteering, walking, and eating dinner?

6 hrs.   15 min.

1:00   7:00 7:15

6 hrs. 15 min.

Perry parks his car at 6:57 P.M. He wants to visit the bookstore, so he puts enough money in the parking meter for 1 hour and 25 minutes. What time should Perry be back at his car?

3 min.   1 hr.   22 min.

6:57 7:00   8:00   8:22

Perry should be back at his car by 8:22 P.M.

Page 85

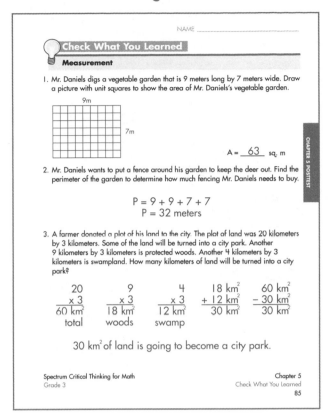

Check What You Learned

Measurement

1. Mr. Daniels digs a vegetable garden that is 9 meters long by 7 meters wide. Draw a picture with unit squares to show the area of Mr. Daniels's vegetable garden.

9m

7m

A = __63__ sq. m

2. Mr. Daniels wants to put a fence around his garden to keep the deer out. Find the perimeter of the garden to determine how much fencing Mr. Daniels needs to buy.

P = 9 + 9 + 7 + 7
P = 32 meters

3. A farmer donated a plot of his land to the city. The plot of land was 20 kilometers by 3 kilometers. Some of the land will be turned into a city park. Another 9 kilometers by 3 kilometers is protected woods. Another 4 kilometers by 3 kilometers is swampland. How many kilometers of land will be turned into a city park?

20	9	4	18 km²	60 km²
$\times 3$	$\times 3$	$\times 3$	$+ 12$ km²	$- 30$ km²
60 km²	18 km²	12 km²	30 km²	30 km²
total	woods	swamp		

30 km² of land is going to become a city park.

Page 86

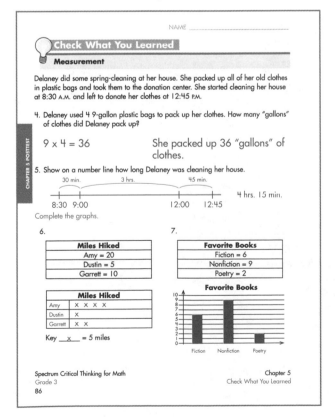

Check What You Learned

Measurement

Delaney did some spring-cleaning at her house. She packed up all of her old clothes in plastic bags and took them to the donation center. She started cleaning her house at 8:30 A.M. and left to donate her clothes at 12:45 P.M.

4. Delaney used 4 9-gallon plastic bags to pack up her clothes. How many "gallons" of clothes did Delaney pack up?

9 x 4 = 36   She packed up 36 "gallons" of clothes.

5. Show on a number line how long Delaney was cleaning her house.

30 min.   3 hrs.   45 min.

8:30 9:00   12:00   12:45   4 hrs. 15 min.

Complete the graphs.

6.

Miles Hiked
Amy = 20
Dustin = 5
Garrett = 10

Miles Hiked				
Amy	X	X	X	X
Dustin	X			
Garrett	X	X		

Key __x__ = 5 miles

7.

Favorite Books
Fiction = 6
Nonfiction = 9
Poetry = 2

Favorite Books

Page 87

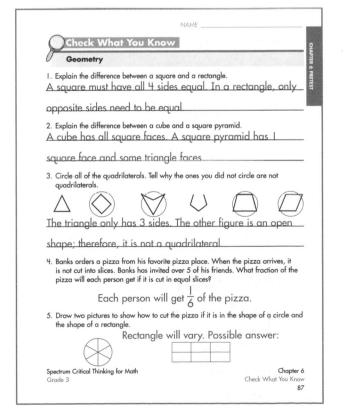

Check What You Know

Geometry

1. Explain the difference between a square and a rectangle.
A square must have all 4 sides equal. In a rectangle, only opposite sides need to be equal.

2. Explain the difference between a cube and a square pyramid.
A cube has all square faces. A square pyramid has 1 square face and some triangle faces.

3. Circle all of the quadrilaterals. Tell why the ones you did not circle are not quadrilaterals.

The triangle only has 3 sides. The other figure is an open shape; therefore, it is not a quadrilateral.

4. Banks orders a pizza from his favorite pizza place. When the pizza arrives, it is not cut into slices. Banks has invited over 5 of his friends. What fraction of the pizza will each person get if it is cut in equal slices?
Each person will get $\frac{1}{6}$ of the pizza.

5. Draw two pictures to show how to cut the pizza if it is in the shape of a circle and the shape of a rectangle.
Rectangle will vary. Possible answer:

Answer Key

Page 88

NAME _____

Lesson 6.1 Plane Figures

A **plane figure** is a flat surface.

circle   triangle   square   rectangle

corner
side
square corner
corner

Each side of a triangle, square, and rectangle is a **line segment**.

The point where two line segments meet is a **corner** or a **square corner**.

A square corner is at a right angle. A right angle has a measure of 90°.

Complete the chart.

	○	▭	△	⬠	⬡
# of sides	0	4	3	5	6
# of square corners	0	4	0	0	0
# of other corners	0	0	3	5	6

Draw a real-world example of two of the shapes above.

Answers will vary.
Possible answers:

YIELD Triangle

SOAP Rectangle

Spectrum Critical Thinking for Math
Grade 3
88

Lesson 6.1
Plane Figures

Page 89

NAME _____

Lesson 6.1 Plane Figures

You can write shape number sentences using shapes and numbers.

A triangle has 3 sides.
3 + 2 = 5
A shape that has five sides is a pentagon.

△ + 2 = ⬠

Solve the following shape number sentences.

⬠ + △ = ○   ⬡ − 2 = ⬠

Create 2 shape number sentences using the shapes below.

○ ▭ ⬡ ▱ ⬠ △

Answers will vary.
Check for accuracy.

Spectrum Critical Thinking for Math
Grade 3

Lesson 6.1
Plane Figures
89

Page 90

NAME _____

Lesson 6.2 Solid Figures

cube   rectangular prism   square pyramid

corner
edge
face
corner
face
corner
edge

A **face** is the shape formed by the edges of a solid figure.

An **edge** is where 2 faces intersect.

A **vertex** or **corner** is the point where 3 or more edges come together.

Complete the table.

	🧊	▱	🔺
# of faces	6	6	5
# of edges	12	12	8
# of vertices	8	8	5

Spectrum Critical Thinking for Math
Grade 3
90

Lesson 6.2
Solid Figures

Page 91

NAME _____

Lesson 6.2 Solid Figures

A baseball is a real-world example of a sphere.

Write the name of the solid figure that each object represents.

🎉	cone
🥫	cylinder
SOAP	rectangular prism

Draw another real-world object that represents a solid shape you have learned about.

Answers will vary.

Spectrum Critical Thinking for Math
Grade 3

Lesson 6.2
Solid Figures
91

124

Answer Key

Page 92

NAME _____

Lesson 6.3 Classifying Quadrilaterals

A trapezoid is a quadrilateral because it has 4 sides. A trapezoid is not a parallelogram because it does not have opposite sides parallel.

A **quadrilateral** is a polygon with 4 sides. Here are some examples:

parallelogram – a quadrilateral with opposite sides parallel

square – rectangle with 4 sides of the same length and all angles equal

rectangle – parallelogram with 4 right angles. Opposite sides are equal.

rhombus – parallelogram with all 4 sides the same length. Opposite angles are the same measure.

kite – 2 pairs of adjacent sides that are congruent

trapezoid – only 2 sides are parallel

Explain how a square can be a quadrilateral, a parallelogram, a rhombus, and a rectangle.

Answers will vary but should reflect the understanding that to be a quadrilateral, there needs to be 4 sides, which a square has. To be a parallelogram, opposite sides need to be parallel, which a square has. To be a rhombus, there needs to be 4 sides of equal length, and 4 angles, which a square has. Lastly, to be a rectangle, there needs to be opposite sides equal, and 4 right angles, which a square also has.

Explain how a rectangle is a quadrilateral and a parallelogram.

Answers will vary but should reflect the understanding that a rectangle is a quadrilateral because it has 4 sides. A rectangle is a parallelogram because it has opposite sides parallel.

Spectrum Critical Thinking for Math
Grade 3
92

Lesson 6.3
Classifying Quadrilaterals

Page 93

NAME _____

Lesson 6.4 Dividing Shapes

Halves = 2 equal pieces
Thirds = 3 equal pieces
Fourths = 4 equal pieces
Fifths = 5 equal pieces
and so on . . .

Divide this shape into thirds.

Label each third.

Answer the questions. Draw pictures to show each answer.

Benjamin is having some friends over for a dinner party. He is having a small rectangle-shaped cake for dessert. He is not sure if one of his 3 friends is going to make it to the dinner party. If all of Benjamin's friends come to the party, how should Benjamin cut the cake so he and his friends can each have an equal piece? If one of the friends does not make it, how should Benjamin cut the cake so he and his friends can each have an equal piece?

Answers will vary.

Possible answer for 4 people:

Possible answer for 3 people:

Mischa bought a large round cheese pizza to share with her family. There are 5 people in her family. Show how Mischa should cut the pizza so that everyone can have one equal piece. Then, show how Mischa should cut the pizza so that everyone can have one equal piece and there is one piece left over.

Equal pieces:

Equal pieces with one left over:

Spectrum Critical Thinking for Math
Grade 3
93

Lesson 6.4
Dividing Shapes

Page 94

NAME _____

Lesson 6.5 Dividing Shapes in the Real World

Solve. Draw a picture to show your thinking.

Grey has a rectangular candy bar. He wants to share it with 3 friends. Draw a picture of the candy bar and show one way Grey can divide it equally with his friends. Label each part with the correct fraction.

Answers will vary.
Possible answer:

| $\frac{1}{4}$ | $\frac{1}{4}$ |
| $\frac{1}{4}$ | $\frac{1}{4}$ |

Show another way Grey can divide the same candy bar, and label it.

Possible answer:

| $\frac{1}{4}$ |
| $\frac{1}{4}$ |
| $\frac{1}{4}$ |
| $\frac{1}{4}$ |

Yolanda is planting a vegetable garden in a square-shaped bed. She wants to plant corn, peppers, squash, and lettuce. She must give each vegetable an equal amount of space in the garden. Draw a diagram that shows how Yolanda's garden can be divided so that all the vegetables get an equal amount of space. Is there another way to divide up the garden? If so, draw and label it.

Answers will vary.
Possible answers:

| corn | peppers |
| lettuce | squash |

or

| $\frac{1}{4}$ |
| $\frac{1}{4}$ |
| $\frac{1}{4}$ |
| $\frac{1}{4}$ |

Spectrum Critical Thinking for Math
Grade 3
94

Lesson 6.5
Dividing Shapes in the Real World

Page 95

NAME _____

💡 **Check What You Learned**

Geometry

1. Mandy and her sister bake a cake to share with their grandmother for her birthday. When Mandy's grandmother first cuts the cake, it is only the 3 of them at her house. However, Grandmother's 3 neighbors come over and would like some cake, too. How can Mandy's grandmother cut the cake now so everyone can have a piece? Draw a picture to show your answer.

First: $\frac{1}{3}$ $\frac{1}{3}$ $\frac{1}{3}$

Now: $\frac{1}{6}$ $\frac{1}{6}$ $\frac{1}{6}$ $\frac{1}{6}$ $\frac{1}{6}$ $\frac{1}{6}$

2. Name the shape that has the following:
   • zero sides
   • zero corners

   circle/sphere

3. Name the shape that has the following:
   • 1 square face
   • 4 triangle faces
   • 0 rectangle faces
   • 8 edges

   square pyramid

4. Circle all the parallelograms. Then, tell why the ones you did not circle are not parallelograms.

   The trapezoid doesn't have opposite, parallel sides. The pentagon has 5 sides, not 4. The other quadrilateral doesn't have any sides parallel.

CHAPTER 6 POSTTEST

Spectrum Critical Thinking for Math
Grade 3
95

Chapter 6
Check What You Learned

Answer Key

Page 96

Final Test Chapters 1–6

Solve the problems. Show your work.

1. There are 983 people who want tickets to a concert. There are 795 tickets available to purchase online. Local radio stations have 75 tickets to give away. How many people will not be able to get tickets?

   $795 + 75 = 870$ 113 people will not be able to
   $983 - 870 = 113$ get tickets.

2. The first 175 people who arrive at the concert will get a free T-shirt. If everyone who wins a ticket from a local radio station will get a free T-shirt, how many people who bought tickets online will get a free T-shirt?

   $175 - 75 = 100$ 100 people who bought tickets will get a free T–shirt.

3. Mr. King has 372 books in his classroom library. Ms. Lewis has 489 books in her classroom library. About how many books do Mr. King and Ms. Lewis have altogether?

   $400 + 500 = 900$ About 900 books

4. About how many more books does Ms. Lewis have than Mr. King?

   $500 - 400 = 100$ About 100 more books

5. Both teachers are allowed to have 500 books in their classroom libraries. Exactly how many more books can each teacher have? Show your work.

   Mr. King: Ms. Lewis:
   $500 - 372 = 128$ books $500 - 489 = 11$ books

Page 97

Final Test Chapters 1–6

Solve the problems. Show your work.

6. Sandra made 4 scarves with 32 feet of fabric. How many feet of fabric would Sandra need to make 35 scarves?

   $32 \div 4 = 8$ She would need 280 feet of fabric.
   $8 \times 35 = 280$

7. April has 12 scarves in her closet. 3 of the scarves are purple, 5 of the scarves are green, and the rest of the scarves have a pattern on them. How many of April's scarves have a pattern on them? Write a fraction for the purple scarves.

   $3 + 5 + ? = 12$ Four of April's scarves have a
   $8 + ? = 12$ pattern on them.
   $12 - 8 = 4$ $\frac{3}{12}$ are purple.

8. Over 10 days, Forrest earns $6 each day for doing household chores. Each day, his mom takes out $3 and puts it into a savings account for Forrest. How much total money does Forrest get to keep?

   $\begin{array}{r} \$6 \\ -\ \$3 \\ \hline \$3 \end{array}$ $\begin{array}{r} 10 \\ \times\ \$3 \\ \hline \$30 \end{array}$ Forrest gets to keep $30.

9. Brian has 63 candies. He wants to put the candy equally into 9 bags. How many candies does Brian need to put in each bag?

   $9\overline{)63}\ ^{7}$ He needs to put 7 candies in each bag.

Page 98

Final Test Chapters 1–6

10. Charlotte bakes 4 coconut cream pies for the bake sale. Norman bakes 4 banana cream pies for the bake sale. Each pie is cut into eighths, and each slice is sold individually. Write a fraction to show the pies Charlotte brings to the bake sale.

    Charlotte brought $\frac{4}{8}$ of the pies to the bake sale.

11. Write a fraction to show the amount of pie that Charlotte and Norman each made.

    $\frac{32}{8}$ coconut cream $\frac{32}{8}$ banana cream

12. Each slice of pie was sold for $2. What was the total cost of a whole pie? Show your work.

    $2 per slice x 8 slices per pie = $16 per pie

13. Show the fraction $\frac{2}{8}$ in three different ways: on a number line, as part of a whole, and as part of a set.

    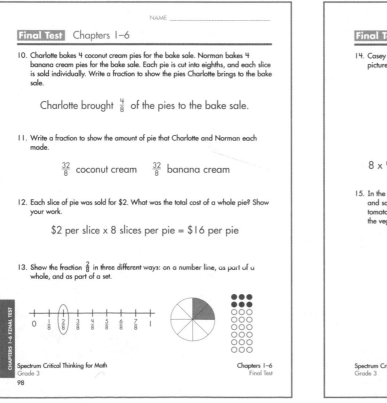

Page 99

Final Test Chapters 1–6

14. Casey plants a vegetable garden that is 8 meters long by 4 meters wide. Draw a picture and find the area of Casey's vegetable garden.

    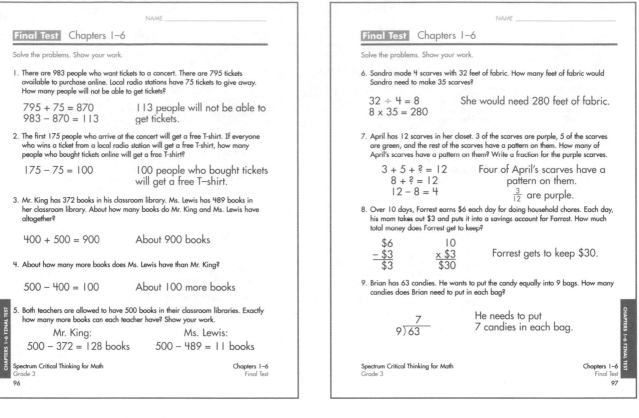

    $8 \times 4 = 32$ $A = 32$ sq. m

15. In the vegetable garden, Casey grows tomatoes, cucumbers, onions, peppers, and squash. By the end of the summer, he has harvested 15 cucumbers, 20 tomatoes, 5 onions, 10 peppers, and 15 squash. Draw a bar graph to show all the vegetables that Casey has harvested.

    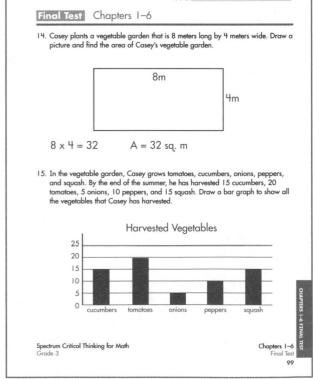

Answer Key

Page 100

Final Test Chapters 1–6

16. Roxanne wants to put a concrete patio behind her house. She wants it to look like the image shown below. The concrete company needs to know the area of the space where she wants her patio so they know how much concrete to pour. Find the area of the space.

$4 \times 2 = 8$
$5 \times 2 = 10$
$8 + 10 = 18$

A = 18 sq ft.

17. Roxanne also wants to put a special trim around the outside edge of the patio. Find the perimeter of the space to determine how much trim Roxanne will need.

$P = 4 + 2 + 2 + 5 + 2 + 7$
$P = 22$ ft.

18. Holly says a baby weighs 8 pounds. Kelsey says a baby weighs 8 ounces. Who is correct? Explain your thinking.

<u>Holly is correct. Ounces are used to describe the weight of a very light object. For example, a bag of potato chips might weigh 8 ounces.</u>

Page 101

Final Test Chapters 1–6

Wyatt tries to drink a lot of water every day. He starts drinking water at 8:30 A.M. every morning, and stops drinking at 8:45 P.M. every evening.

19. Wyatt drinks 36 ounces before noon, and 36 ounces after noon. How many ounces does Wyatt drink altogether?

$\begin{array}{r} 36 \\ + 36 \\ \hline 72 \end{array}$ Wyatt drinks 72 ounces altogether.

20. Show on a number line how long Wyatt drinks water every day.

30 min.   11 hrs.   45 min.

8:30   9:00   8:00   8:45

12 hrs. 15 min.

21. The following chart shows how many total ounces of water Wyatt drank over the past 3 days. Draw a picture graph to show the information in the chart.

Water (Ounces)	
Day 1	70
Day 2	80
Day 3	65

Key = 🥛 = 10 ounces

Amount of Water Drank

Day 1	🥛🥛🥛🥛🥛🥛🥛
Day 2	🥛🥛🥛🥛🥛🥛🥛🥛
Day 3	🥛🥛🥛🥛🥛🥛🥤

Page 102

Final Test Chapters 1–6

22. As a treat, Ms. Rizzo makes a giant cookie shaped like a triangle. She divides her students into 3 groups with 2 people in each group. Then, she cuts the cookie into 3 pieces. She gives each group a piece. Ms. Rizzo tells each group they need to divide their piece so that each person gets a piece. Draw a picture to show how Ms. Rizzo divided the giant triangle cookie for the whole club. Then draw a picture to show how each group divided their cookie.

Ms. Rizzo: Each group:

23. Brad tells Shelby that a trapezoid is a parallelogram, but not a quadrilateral. Shelby is unsure. Is Brad right? Explain your answer.

<u>Brad is wrong. A trapezoid is a quadrilateral because it has 4 sides. But it is not a parallelogram because its sides are not parallel.</u>

24. Name both figures shown. Explain how they are the same and how they are different.

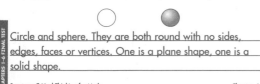

<u>Circle and sphere. They are both round with no sides, edges, faces or vertices. One is a plane shape, one is a solid shape.</u>

Notes